Miss Match

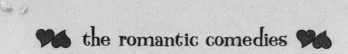
the romantic comedies

Miss Match

WENDY TOLIVER

Simon Pulse

New York London Toronto Sydney

SIMON PULSE
An imprint of Simon & Schuster Children's Publishing Division
1230 Avenue of the Americas, New York, NY 10020
Copyright © 2009 by Wendy Toliver
All rights reserved, including the right of reproduction in whole or in part in any form.
SIMON PULSE and colophon are registered trademarks of Simon & Schuster, Inc.
Designed by Ann Zeak
The text of this book was set in Garamond 3.
Manufactured in the United States of America
First Simon Pulse paperback edition February 2009
10 9 8 7 6 5 4 3 2 1
Library of Congress Control Number 2008929573
ISBN-13: 978-1-4169-6413-1
ISBN-10: 1-4169-6413-4

For Matt, my perfect match

Acknowledgments

This being my second Simon Pulse novel, I'd first like to thank those who've embraced *The Secret Life of a Teenage Siren*. Your support means the world to me. All my gratitude to my agents, Christina Hogrebe and Annelise Robey, for their guidance and enthusiasm, and to my editor, Michael del Rosario, who made *Miss Match* truly shine. Thanks to Caroline Abbey and the rest of the Simon & Schuster team—both past and present—for having faith in me, right from the start. God has blessed me with the most loving friends and family. I wouldn't be able to follow my dream if they weren't always standing behind me. I'm also blessed with the most amazing CPs: the Eden Writers Circle, Kwana, Nadine, Aryn, Kristin, and Jennifer. I'm grateful to Mom and Penny for making it possible for occasional escapes. Three cheers for Marley and Drienie, who keep me going strong, and Matt, who attempts to keep me sane. Big hugs to Anna, the sweetest girl in the universe, and Miller, Collin, and Dawson, who will be my babies forever.

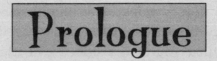

Prologue

Bam!

My head slams into the headrest of my seat. Oh no. *No!*

I clench my eyes shut and slowly turn around, afraid to see what I've hit. By the time I open my eyes again, a lump the size of Jupiter has taken residence in my throat.

Mrs. Woosely jumps out of her car and claps her hands over her mouth. I shift into park, turn off the ignition, and race over to her on wobbly legs. Mrs. Woosely has lived down the street from us as long as I can remember, in the house with all the plastic pink flamingoes poked into the flowerbed. One Halloween when I was, like, seven, my best friend, Yasmin, and I transplanted her flamingoes to the churchyard on the next block. We thought it was hilarious.

But this, *this* isn't the least bit funny.

"I'm so sorry, Mrs. Woosely," I say, trying to keep from bawling. "Are you okay?"

She does a remarkable impression of a fish: lips pursed together, eyes bugged out, hands flittering at her sides like little fins. "Yes, I'm all right." After blowing out a long, loud stream of air she examines the dent in the side of her little white Toyota. "Can't say the same for my car, though."

How could this have happened to me? So close to getting my license. So close to getting my very own car. My own independence! And now look what I've done. *Argh!* I am sooooo dead.

"Mrs. Woosely, I'm *so* sorry about this. I was just moving my dad's truck so, you know, I could play basketball, and I—"

"I know you're sorry, dear. I'm going to be late for my dialysis, though. So let's exchange insurance information and I'll be on my way."

I brush my hand along the bumper of Dad's SUV. Miraculously, there's only a little scratch. Might even be undetectable.

Wait a minute.

Turning around, I scan the windows of the house. No signs of witnesses.

What if Dad never finds out about this accident?

"About that, Mrs. Woosely. You see . . ." I give the flamingo aficionada one of my sweetest, most sincere smiles. "Well, I guess what I'm asking is, if I promise to pay for the repairs, do you think you can keep this whole thing under wraps? My parents are already so upset with their divorce and everything, and I'd hate to distress them even more. You know?"

Mrs. Woosely paces up and down the length of her car, the asphalt crunching under her tasseled loafers. Her white curls are so tight they don't even flutter in the March breeze. Finally, she says, "Well, I suppose that would be all right. My son just went through a horrible divorce himself. Now, I don't really approve of divorces, because I figure when you make a promise to God . . . but then again God didn't intend for men to marry hussies who cavort with other men half their age, either."

She stops and looks at me, a tinge of pity in her light gray eyes. She chuckles softly and puts her hand on my shoulder. "I'm sorry, dear. Don't mind me. I'm an old woman with too many opinions." She turns and opens the door to her car, then winks at me over her shoulder. "I'll have it fixed and hand you the bill. It'll be our secret." Mrs. Woosely presses her finger to her lips and then folds her petite body into the driver's seat.

After her wounded car disappears around the bend, I carefully pull the SUV back up the driveway and then head inside the house. Mom and Dad are sitting on the couch in the living room, a vast expanse of worn-in leather separating them. The instant they hear me, Dad clears his throat meaningfully, and Mom concentrates on centering her glass on its coaster. Mom's glass is filled to the rim with iced tea; Dad's is half empty. I feel squished by the weight of their silence as they turn and give me flimsy *everything's okay* smiles.

As far as I can tell, they didn't witness the accident. I'm sure Dad would've said something by now. I hand him his keys.

Clearing his throat again, Dad half stands. "You sure didn't play very long, Sasha," he says, stuffing the keys into his pocket and then lowering his body onto the couch again. "You didn't have any trouble moving my truck, did you?"

I blink, not really sure what to say. Did they see the accident after all? Are they just waiting for me to come clean? My cheeks, which were wind-chilled only moments ago, now feel like they're about to melt off my face.

"Everything all right, Sasha?" Mom asks softly.

Shrugging in a way I hope appears non-chalant, I say, "Just got bored, you know, shooting hoops all alone." Then, as soon as I can slink away without being totally rude, I escape up the stairs and into my bedroom, leaving my parents alone to discuss the finer points of their so-called amicable divorce. As I look out the window at Dad's SUV, I get a gnawing feeling in the pit of my stomach.

I'm totally relieved my parents didn't see me crash into Mrs. Woosely's car. But how am I going to keep it a secret from them? And even if they never find out, how am I going to make enough money to pay for the car repair?

Eight hundred dollars.

Eight hundred dollars.

I'm sure my eyes are popping out of their sockets as I read Mrs. Woosely's Jiffy Auto

Body Repair statement. Will I be shackled to this debt for the rest of my high school years? It's all too clear that I have to do something major. I've got to come up with a way to make some mega bucks, and fast.

But what? It's not that I have anything against the Gap or McDonald's, but it'll take an *eternity* to earn eight hundred bucks doing a minimum-wage-type job.

I rack my brain for something that I'm good at, something I enjoy. You know, kinda like those fill-in-the-bubble career aptitude tests we're forced to take at school. Or the "Which Career Matches Your Personality?" quizzes on Seventeen.com.

After five minutes of hitting dead ends I reach for the phone and dial Yasmin's number.

"If you were a career counselor, what kind of job would you recommend for me?" I ask after she answers.

"So your dad's making you get a job? I told you things would be different once he moved in with his girlfriend. Things always are."

"A job, Yas. What kind of job would I be good at?" I say, trying to steer her back on course. I click the remote and my TV comes to life. It's one of those lame after-school specials. Two teenage girls are trying to get the attention of a guy in a leather jacket. The brunette chick is really into him, but he isn't giving her the time of day. She's failing miserably, doing everything she shouldn't and nothing she should. If I could just pop into the television and work a little magic, I'd have that guy dying to ask her out . . .

"Matchmaker," Yas says.

"Come again?"

"You're a natural-born matchmaker, Sasha."

I turn off the TV and ponder this for a moment.

"Remember how you fixed up Jarren and Caitlyn Sparks?" she asks.

I laugh. "That was, like, the first grade!" Jarren told me he thought Caitlyn was cute and wondered if she liked him back. Something came over me. I *had* to help get these two together. I snuck out to the hall and moved his Batman backpack next to her Disney Princess one. The next day I had everybody shuffle around so they'd be sitting next to each other for circle time. Two days later he was sharing his Little Debbie with Caitlyn at lunch and gave her a picture he'd drawn of her—both suggestions of mine. By the end of the week I saw them holding hands at recess. I was more excited than he was!

"Do you think people would pay me to fix them up with their crushes?" I ask. Matchmaking has always been a hobby of mine. Could I actually earn money doing it?

"Absolutely." While Yas delves into a monologue about different cultures and their commitment to matchmakers and how America could use a personal touch in this era of Internet dating and virtual sex (whatever that means), I make a big decision.

I'll be the world's first teenage matchmaker. Or at least the first one in northern Utah.

After I thank my friend and hang up, I begin plowing through the articles about boys and dating and falling in love that I've clipped from magazines. I watch the movies and talk shows about matchmaking that I've recorded through the years. Then, hopped-up on inspiration and adrenaline, I pluck away on my laptop into the wee hours of the night.

By the time the sun pops up, I, Sasha Finnegan, have been reborn as Miss Match. Watch out, Cupid, there's a new matchmaker in town!

One

I spit a jaw-achingly huge gob of bubble gum into my palm and look at my watch. Three . . . two . . . one. The shrill ring pierces throughout Snowcrest High School, sending the last few students scurrying to their first-period classes.

The hall is as vacant as the library-sponsored Don't Forget to Read During the Summer popcorn-and-punch party last May. By that I mean no one's out here except for Mrs. Leonard (the librarian) and *moi*.

Um, yeah. I was there. But only 'cause I was trying to fix up our school's And Literacy For All chapter prez with her crush. Neither of whom showed up. Which explains why Mrs. Leonard thinks I'm some sort of superdevout bookworm who just loves volunteering in the periodicals section. I can already tell that my locker placement—right next to the library— is going to prove problematic. Hoping she doesn't notice me (and heaven forbid venture over for a chitchat) I pretend to be searching for something in my locker. Only it's the first day of school, so besides a tiny magnetic mirror, a tube of Kiss & Tell lip gloss, and my reserve of loose-leaf paper, the locker's empty.

Mrs. Leonard's trademark blue suede pumps *clack-clack* back into her bookly haven, and I relax. By now my gum has started to harden, so I pop it back in my mouth, give it a good thorough chew, and divide it in half with my tongue and teeth.

One more glance to ensure the coast is clear, and I stick the gum wads in the doorjamb of my locker, one up top and one below. Then I shut the door, squeezing it firmly closed.

After a few seconds I do the combo and try to open my locker. It won't budge. I try again, wiggling it more forcefully. No luck.

Here's the plan: Anna Black (my client's crush) will be trying to get her locker unstuck (after I've performed Operation Gum Stick to it), and right when she's starting to freak out about getting her first-ever tardy mark, Hunter Davidson (my client) will show up like a knight in shining armor to successfully open it. Naturally, she'll bat her eyelashes, swoon, and sigh a heartfelt "My hero." And they'll live happily ever after.

Okay, maybe it won't happen *exactly* like that, but it will definitely put Hunter on her radar and make a terrific first impression. That's a big step in the whole process. *Huge*, actually. And yes, maybe this whole scenario sounds a bit old-fashioned, but I've had my matchmaking business for six months now, and if you ask any of my male clients, bringing chivalry back definitely has its rewards.

I kick my locker. Still won't open. Hmmm.

"Need a hand?" It's a soft Southern drawl, and when I whirl around, I'm half expecting to see Matthew McConaughey. Had it really been Matthew, I don't think I'd be any less spellbound. The guy standing before me—tall, longish sandy-colored hair, dark blue eyes with long lashes, sexy smile, a dimple in his left cheek . . . *erm*. What did he say? Oh yeah.

"Sure. Thanks." I scratch my head while he wrestles with the locker. "I have no clue why the darn thing keeps sticking on me. Guess I'll have to find the janitor."

"Naw," he says, examining the doorjamb. "I'm fixin' to get it." He takes his leather wallet out of his back pocket, unfolds it, and extracts a toothpick. Then he proceeds to poke at the top of the locker door, where I stuck one wad of gum. The gum loosens, and he continues jiggling and joggling the door until it flies open.

"Did you put that there?" he asks, pointing at the gum that's still stuck to the bottom part of the jamb. (I don't even want to think about where the other piece ended up.)

Oh, the humility. I just love admitting I'm crazy to hot new guys. "Well, it was kind of an experiment," I say, fully realizing how lame that sounds. "For a class," I add, in case he thinks I am doing the proverbial damsel-in-distress thing to meet a guy. Sure, I stage these types of things all the time so my clients can get with their crushes, but I wouldn't use such tactics myself.

And it turns out I won't be using this particular tactic to help Hunter, either. Mark Operation Gum Stick a failure.

Maybe if I stuff some paper in the jamb . . . ?

"Well, thanks for the help," I say, realizing that The Hot New Guy is just standing there, staring at me. What, do I have something in my nose? Or lipstick on my tooth? I'm not really used to wearing lipstick, but my sister, Maddie, just got a new shade and insisted I try it out when she drove me to school this morning.

"No problem." He turns to leave, and I take this opportunity to check myself in the locker mirror. Hmm. Nose and tooth check clear.

"Hey! You're new around here, right?" I know I'm stating the obvious, but at least it might postpone his vanishing act. And boy, I could definitely use a little more of this eye candy. Besides, I'm already late, and there's no difference between a little late and a lot late on one's attendance record.

"Just moved here from Texas," he says, walking backward so he can face me.

"Cool." I twirl my hair around my finger. Does it look as cute when I do this as when Maddie does it? Probably not, since her gorgeous auburn mane doesn't know the meaning of Bad Hair Day, while my just-long-enough-for-a-ponytail brown hair—*not* chestnut or nutmeg or pecan or hazelnut or walnut or espresso or chocolate or any of those deluxe (and suspiciously yummy-sounding) colors—could very well be the founder and president. Of Bad Hair Day, that is.

"I guess so," The Hot New Guy says. "Well, I'll see ya around. Gotta get to class. And next time you need a place to put your gum, try a trash can."

"Right. Of course. No problem. See you. Bye." Please tell me that dreadful giggling isn't spewing out of my mouth.

He swaggers (he actually *swaggers*!) down the hall and disappears into the east wing. Which is just as well, because I should probably be getting to class myself.

I gather my chemistry book and folder and scurry down the hall to room 116. Mr. Foley is writing something on the blackboard, and for a split second I frolic in the belief that I'm getting off scot-free. But as I slip into an empty seat in the back, he twirls around and pegs me with an *I caught you* glare. I swallow and then smile, hoping I'm the essence of innocence. Mr. Foley glances down at a piece of paper on his desk—the class roster, I presume?—and says, "And you are . . . ?"

This is my second semester with Mr. Foley (he also teaches driver's ed), so you'd think he'd know who I am by now. But I guess I'm not surprised. I'm pretty good at blending in. Maybe that's why I'm so good at my job. A flamboyant, center-stage type would have a hard time keeping her identity under wraps, I'd think.

"Sasha Finnegan." I don't have a perfect record like Anna Black does at her school, but still, it's a little embarrassing to be put on the spot like this. And the instant I catch a glimpse of a familiar sandy-haired, blue-eyed, Texas-A&M-T-shirted guy in the second row, my embarrassment modifier jumps to *totally*.

Mr. Foley makes a gross guttural noise and says, "If it's okay with you, Sasha, I'd like to start class *on time* from now on."

"Yes, sir," I say, squirming in my seat.

Mr. Foley launches into a lecture, but it's impossible to concentrate on all those formulas and definitions. Didn't he get the memo that today is all about fun and games? Who ever heard of a teacher who makes his students actually *work* on the first day of school? While he yammers on, I keep looking out the window. Not that there's anything interesting happening in the juniper bush out there, but if I tilt my head just so, I have an excellent peripheral view of The Hot New Guy.

My faith in the minute hand is restored when the bell rings and we all gather our folders and backpacks. "Go directly to the gym for the back-to-school assembly," Mr. Foley calls over the din.

I look for The Hot New Guy in the hall. (I'll just call him THNG until I figure out his name.) But, apparently, the swarm of high schoolers has swallowed him whole. Any other day I'd skip the gaudy spectacle of school spirit otherwise known as the pep rally, but Maddie's been working really hard on her routine, and what kind of sister would I be to miss her debut as varsity cheerleader? And since THNG is new and naive and everything, he'll probably be at the pep rally. Not that I'm stalking him.

Squinting, I leave the fluorescent-lit hallway and enter the sunshiny brightness of the gymnasium. The freshly buffed wooden court gleams, and a collage of hand-painted banners scream *Snowcrest Rams Rule!* and

SHS is #1! from the walls. The enormous room is buzzing with first-day-of-school exuberance.

"Sasha! Over here!"

Twisting around, I spot Yasmin waving frantically from the tip-top of the bleachers. As usual she's dressed to thrill, her first-day-of-school ensemble consisting of pin-striped trouser shorts and a red satin wraparound top à la Hilary Duff at the Teen Choice Awards.

I muscle my way up the steps and "excuse me, pardon me, *ouch*!" my way to her side. "Why do you always have to sit in the nosebleed section?" I ask, slightly out of breath. How she climbed all those stairs in three-inch heels, I'll never know.

"'Cause I get to scam all the hot guys," she answers, not even caring that the boys sitting around us are all listening in. She tucks her shiny black hair behind a thoroughly adorned ear and says, "Oh my God, Sasha. You look darling. Where'd you get that skirt?"

I have to look to remember what I'm wearing. Right. It's Tommy Hilfiger, and it flares out a little on the bottom. The flare part makes my thighs look a little less . . .

well, a little *less*. "Maddie's closet," I say. "But it falls off of her, so she bequeathed it to me." Sure, I can fit into a few of Maddie's sweatshirts and shoes, but it's not every day I can say I'm wearing something of hers. I should be psyched about scoring a brand-new, this-season skirt, but what I wouldn't give to be the Skinny Sister for once.

Yas nods understandingly. "Yeah, that super-stretchy denim can be totally misleading. She should've bought one two sizes smaller than what she normally wears." Then she faces forward and says, "Oh, look. It's starting!"

First, the student body is treated to the procession of teachers and teachers' aides, who march solemnly across the court and file into the front few rows. Next, this year's starched-and-pressed student council parades in, treating their subjects to a sequence of waves, thumbs-up, fist pumps, and one particularly jarring fingers-in-mouth whistle. I feel a headache coming on. And when the marching band makes its big entrance, banging and clanging out something that sounds roughly like the Snowcrest High School fight song, I wonder: Can a headache spread to one's whole body?

Yasmin elbows me and gestures (not very

subtly) at a potential hottie. He's sitting on the ground level, so it's not like I could see what he looks like even if he were facing us. But the back of his head looks pretty cute, so I smile and nod, wishing there were a volume control on the band. Yasmin bites her lower lip as that *I'm gonna get him* gleam settles in her exotic eyes.

The JV cheerleaders take center stage in their new black-and-red uniforms, doing round-offs and aerials and complicated twisty-tricks as they shout, "Goooooo, Snowcrest!" Then they reach out their arms and give the spirit-fingers salute to the varsity squad, who's hot on their trail. Launching into their routine, which is thankfully accompanied by a CD and not the marching band, the varsity cheerleaders fling their tiny bodies around in perfect time.

They're . . . *good*. Great, even. I can't take my eyes off of them.

And Maddie looks the best of all. She's zipping through her back handsprings like she has actual springs growing out of her feet. Oh my God, did she just do a whip back? And now she's being launched to the tip-top of a pyramid. All those cheerleader camps have really paid off!

"Maddie looks amazing," Yas says, pointing at my sis as if I need help locating her. Just look around. *Everybody* is checking her out.

Then I notice him. THNG. He's sitting four rows in front of me, two o'clock. I can see from here that he's zeroed in on Maddie. Is that a trickle of drool on his chin? Well, I shouldn't be surprised. I mean, Maddie is drop-dead gorgeous—all silky auburn hair, green eyes, and freakishly long legs. If she weren't my sister, I'd definitely hate her.

Maddie does a dead man, falling backward into three other cheerleaders' hands. Then they pitch her up and she does another dead man, forward. The student body goes wild as she pops up and flings her hair back into place. She joins the others in their little "Go! Fight! Win!" cheer. It looks like Maddie Finnegan has given Snowcrest High a terrible case of school spirit. I just hope the whole place doesn't have to be quarantined.

As soon as Yasmin drops me off at my house, I grab a snack and run up to my room. I shuck my sweater and sprawl out on my bed. I get out my laptop and write a quick update e-mail to Hunter, letting him know a brilliant plan is in the works and to hang tight for further direction. After I hit send, I notice there's a message in my inbox waiting to be opened.

Subj: Request 4 Help
Date: Sept. 9, 2:47 PM Mountain Standard Time
From: 66Chevy@kmail.com
To: MissMatch@MissMatch4Hire.com

Dear Miss Match,

My friend Caden Baxter told me about you. You really came thru for him and I'm hoping you can work the same magic for me?

Here's the deal. There's a girl at my school. Not just any girl—she's a goddess. I want to ask her to the homecoming dance, but I doubt she even knows I exist. Anyway, homecoming is only a month away, so I know I'm asking a lot. I'll pay you extra. Let me know.

Thanks,
Derek Urban

Derek's e-mail isn't anything out of the ordinary. I get e-mails like this every week. It's all part of the job. But when I start reading the

Miss Match Questionnaire he so kindly filled out in full, I about fall off my bed. I blink three times and reread the first line:

NAME OF CRUSH: Maddie Finnegan

This Derek guy wants me to fix him up with *my sister*!

I've worked wonders with beauties and beasts, princes and paupers, city mice and country mice, angels and devils . . . but never anything so close to home. Literally.

Sure, since I work locally (it's not like I can jet set all over the world) there's always the chance I'll know or recognize a client or the person he or she is all into. But I never thought I'd see the day that a guy would pay me to fix him up with my own flesh-and-blood sister.

Who is this Derek guy, anyway? Am I going to like him enough to help him get a date with my sister? And who's to say Maddie will even give him the time of day? Does he realize that she's dated the dreamiest guys from Provo to Logan, and one who just left for his sophomore year at Yale? Or that Maddie changes boyfriends as often as she changes her Abercrombie & Fitch jeans?

Then again, he *did* offer to pay me extra,

and after six long months I'm only one gig away from clearing my debt to Mrs. Woosely once and for all. Besides, when have I ever backed down from a challenge? I guess I can always refund his money and refuse to make the match if I don't feel right about it . . . right? So really, what's to lose?

I'll just have to get to know this Derek Urban before I fix him up with Maddie.

I hit reply and type:

Subj: Important Message from M.M.
Date: Sept. 9, 10:03 PM Mountain Standard Time
From: MissMatch@MissMatch4Hire.com
To: 66Chevy@kmail.com

Dear Derek,

Greetings, and congratulations on finding Miss Match. You're about to embark on a romantic adventure, and I'm here to provide the magic to get it all started.

Meet me at Subway at noon on Friday. Since homecoming's just around the corner, every minute counts. I'll be wearing a red T-shirt with a white heart.

Ciao for now,
M.M.

*

It's Friday, 11:54 a.m. I'm sitting in the far corner of the hard yellow booth at the Subway across the street from Snowcrest. It smells like yeast and onions in here. The September sun blares through the window and penetrates my scalp. High schoolers roll in and out, but no one pays any attention to me.

My cell phone rings. It's Yasmin. "Where are you?" she asks.

Ugh. I'm such a bad friend. "I'm sorry, girl. I totally spaced eating with you. I'm actually having a working lunch today."

Ever since the day she suggested I turn my matchmaking hobby into an actual moneymaking profession, Yasmin has been my loyal and fabulous sidekick. Not only is she the reigning yearbook editor, she has a flair for digging up everything and anything that's scandalicious. She's an expert secret- and gossip-miner. Seriously. I'm floored with all the "news" she's privy to. Plus, while I tend to blend in, she's a hottie with a look-at-me attitude, and that proves useful from time to time. Miss Match wouldn't be such a success if it weren't for Yas.

"Sure, just stand me up. What, am I supposed to eat alone?" she says with a slight whine in her voice. "Might as well banish me to Loserdom."

"Maybe you can go with Hilary and Sami?" I suggest. "They're probably at Arctic Circle."

"Okay. Oh, wait. Brian's waving at me. Maybe he'll split his PB&J with me."

"Sounds yummy."

"Yeah, I love peanut butter."

"No, I mean Brian." I've always thought Yas and Brian would make the perfect couple, and I'm even more sure of it now. Long gone are the lanky limbs and pimples of yesteryear. The summer's been good to him, and Yas noticed too. "Did you know Brian's the hottie you were checking out at the pep rally?" I ask.

After a pause, she says, "Really? That's weird."

"There's no denying he's looking *good* these days, Yas."

"Yeah, I guess you're right." Her voice sounds a bit distant, like she's holding her phone away from her mouth. "Well, I'd better let you go, so you can work."

We hang up just as someone slides up to the booth, hovering over me. Oh my God, it's THNG. "Hi!" he says, putting his hands on the table and leaning forward.

I'm sure I've got some major red-face issues just about now. Man, he's cute. He's wearing baggy, olive-colored shorts and flip-flops. I can't help but notice what nice legs he has: long and muscular with a leftover summer tan. He leans down and whispers in my ear, "So, what's up, Miss Match?" *Oooooh*, that accent!

Hang on.

Did he just call me . . . ? No way. THNG is Derek Urban? THNG wants me to fix him up with my sister?

My jaw falls to the floor.

Two

Get a grip, Sasha.

Why am I so surprised that he's the one? I saw him drooling over Maddie at the pep rally. Plus, he's new in town and probably doesn't know a lot of people around here. It's only natural he'd want to take the hottest girl in school to homecoming, right?

I clear my throat and hold out my hand, hoping it's not all sweaty. "Just call me Sasha. You know, in public."

He takes my hand and shakes it slowly. His dark blue eyes are hypnotic. "Do I know you?" he asks.

"We have chemistry together. Er—the class, I mean." Oh, God. "I usually sit in the back, but maybe you've seen me there?"

He nods. "Maybe." He stretches the two-syllable word into four with his soft drawl.

"And you also helped me get my locker unstuck," I blather on.

"That's right. I remember." But he says it in a way that makes me wonder if he really does remember, or if he's just saying so to be nice. Then again, if he did forget the whole Operation Gum Stick experiment, I'm totally relieved. Which reminds me, I need to do some more tweaking on that particular plan for Hunter.

"So, whatcha havin'?" THNG—I mean, Derek—asks, jerking his thumb at the sandwich line.

"Uh, nothing. I'm not hungry."

"You've gotta eat lunch, Sasha. Feed your brain."

"More like feed my thighs," I mutter.

He looks under the table. "There's nothing wrong with your thighs."

Oh, God. I feel like my head is going to spontaneously combust. I squeeze out a snort sound, praying my face isn't as red as my shirt. "Um, why don't you get yourself a sandwich? Then we'll go somewhere else, so we can talk."

He hops up and stands under the big

PLACE ORDER HERE sign. When it's his turn, I hear him order a Footlong Club Fresh Value Meal. "Hey, Sasha! You sure you don't want a Coke or a bag of Doritos?" he calls across the restaurant. "How about a chocolate chip cookie?" He points to the plastic cookie container on the counter and licks his lips like he's in a cheesy commercial.

I smile and shake my head no. Okay, so I lied when I said I wasn't hungry. I'm always hungry, and a meatball sandwich sounds way good right now. But in a moment of wishful thinking I squished into my skinny jeans this morning, and they'll burst if I eat anything. Plus, I have this weird thing about eating in front of guys.

I guess I shouldn't think of Derek as a guy. I mean, he's my client. *If* I find him worthy of my sister, that is.

After Derek gets his lunch, we walk back across the street to Snowcrest's track and settle on the peeling green bleachers. There's a hint of an autumn breeze in the air, but it's warm and sunny. I love September. The weather's perfect, the aspen leaves are turning yellow, and it's my birthday month. I can't believe it—just three more days till I'm sixteen!

A black Eclipse whizzes by, bass pounding. We watch it turn into the student parking lot and disappear down a row of cars. I can't wait till I have my own set of wheels and don't have to always rely on my parents, Maddie, and Yas for rides.

Derek unwraps his sandwich and takes a bite. With his mouth full he mumbles, "So why'd we meet at Subway and then come back here?"

"I have to be extra careful that no one knows what I do." I lower my voice, even though there's no one around. "Can't blow my cover. Besides, I wanted to make sure you'd get to eat some lunch. You can't ask Maddie Finnegan to homecoming with a growling stomach."

"Not only are you sneaky, you're considerate." He waves his club sandwich in the air. "Want a bite?"

"No, really. But thanks."

He takes a huge bite and chews with his lips slightly parted. The lump in his cheek quickly disappears, and then he swallows, his Adam's apple shimmying. "So, tell me what I need to do."

I blink. Right. Maddie.

I guess there *might* be a chance for him.

With Maddie, I mean. First of all, he's so cute. Second, Maddie wouldn't know Derek Urban from George Washington. Which would definitely work to his advantage. If he's a geek or a jerk or a nose picker or an ax murderer, she'd be none the wiser. For all Maddie knows, he could've been the crown jewel of whatever Bible Belt high school he came from—a varsity jacket flung over his shoulder, a prom-king crown dangling from his fingertips, and a cell phone that all the Southern belles call nonstop. Ah, I can see it now . . .

But wait. This is my sister we're talking about. What if he *is* a murderer?

"Are you okay?" he asks, popping open his Big Grab. "You look like there's something stuck in your throat."

"You've never killed anyone, right?" Oh my God. I didn't just say that out loud, did I? "Uh, that's not what I meant to say. Sorry. What I meant was, you've never asked Maddie out, right?"

He tosses a couple of chips into his mouth and grins as he crunches. "Nope. I don't think she even knows me. That's why I need your help."

"Yes, of course," I say. "You read my

matchmaking philosophy on my website, right?"

"Yes, ma'am." He clears his throat and recites all officially, "You've got to put yourself in the picture."

I smile. "Right. I'd hate to think how many could-be love connections never happen 'cause the one with the crush just watches all googly-eyed from the sidelines."

"Well, Miss Match, I'm ready to stop watching all googly-eyed from the sidelines and put myself in the picture."

I laugh. "Great! Let's get started, then." Then I pause, knowing what I've got to get out in the open before this goes any further. "Listen, Derek," I say, now serious. "There's something I need to be honest with you about, from the start."

"All right. Shoot."

"Maddie's my sister."

His eyes widen. "Ah. Now I see the resemblance."

I snort. When most people learn that Maddie and I are sisters, they assume one of us was adopted. No one's *ever* said we resemble each other in any way whatsoever. Since she was born fifteen months before me, she selfishly used up all of Mom and Dad's top-quality genes. Oh, I know I shouldn't complain. Maddie really is a great sister. And she deserves a great boyfriend. Maybe, possibly, Derek is the One.

"So, if you two are sisters, I guess this makes . . . *this* . . . pretty awkward." Derek peers down at his sandwich and hunches his shoulders a little.

"Not at all." I flash my best confident saleswoman's smile—the one I picked up from Mom when she's trying to close a real-estate deal. "As far as I'm concerned, I have an edge. I know exactly what makes my sister tick, and I can help you become the guy she's dying to go to homecoming with." Oh, wow. There's that dimple. I hope Maddie likes dimples. "So, here's the plan," I continue. "You're in chemistry, so I take it you passed algebra with flying colors?"

"Well, I guess . . . but it's been forever ago."

I shake my head. "No matter. You see, Maddie's terrible at algebra. If she doesn't keep a 3.0 GPA, she'll be kicked off the cheerleading squad. So, I'm going to tell her you're the school's top algebra tutor. She'll show up at the library to meet you. How does four o'clock on Wednesday sound?

There aren't any games that night, so I think all she has is cheerleader practice, which wraps up at three forty-five."

"Wednesday at four. Okay, I'll be there. But I've never tutored anybody before."

"Just help her with her homework . . ." I trail off, distracted by a bread crumb on his lower lip.

". . . and be myself?" he fills in the blank, grinning.

"No! Er, no. I mean, you want to be yourself to some extent, but if you want to impress her, you've got to go beyond that."

"Really?" His grin deflates a couple of notches.

"You know, embrace her values as your own. Show her that you two have a lot in common. But you've got to be somewhat mysterious, too. Don't give her all the answers. Make her work a little. You've got to leave her wanting more."

He cocks an eyebrow. "I'm confused here."

"Let's start with the easy part. Tell me about yourself."

"I'm from Paris, Texas—"

"Stop. Maybe leave out the Texas part. Paris is much more glamorous."

"*Oui*. But I don't exactly pass for a Frenchman, Sasha."

"She'll never know. Besides, it's not lying."

"I guess not . . ."

"What else? What do you do for fun?"

"Ride."

"A Harley?" I ask hopefully.

"My horse. Bob."

"Oh. Well that works, I suppose. She has a My Pretty Pony from when she was, like, seven. It's pink. What else?"

"I play the guitar."

"Are you in a band?"

He scratches his shoulder. "A one-man band."

"Hmm."

"I work on my truck. It's a 1966 Chevy. It was my grandpa's, back in the day." Oooh. I love old pickups. But Maddie won't appreciate its inherent charm. She'll wonder why it hasn't been taken to the junkyard yet.

"Do you know anyone who has a *cool* car? You know, something like a Viper? Or even a Mustang, perhaps?"

"No, why?"

"Erm, never mind. Okay, let's talk about Maddie now." I dig a red spiral notebook and pen out of my backpack and slide it across to him. "Take notes."

"Okay." He holds his pen in ready-to-write position and looks up at me expectantly.

"Her favorite flower is a daisy. Yellow. She once saw an episode of *Gilmore Girls* where a man proposed to Lorelai by filling her house with a thousand yellow daisies, and she still talks about it."

"Yellow daisies. Check."

"She loves old New Wave music like Depeche Mode. But she'd never admit it 'cause she's into what people think of her."

"Closet New Waver. Check." Without looking up from the notepad he asks, "She doesn't have a boyfriend, does she?"

"Uh, she dates a lot of guys"—he looks up at me and blinks—"but usually breaks it off after a month or so."

"Why?"

I shrug. "Not sure. Maybe she's afraid of commitment. Or maybe she's got ADD or something. But the good news is, she's not in a serious relationship. So she's as good as yours."

"Hmm."

"Her favorite cologne is Polo Explorer. She's always stopping at the counter in

Dillard's and sniffing the sample cards. I recommend you get your hands on some, if at all possible. It'll totally turn her on."

"Well, I'm pretty well stocked in the cologne department, but I don't know. Maybe I can try it out."

"Good. Okay, let's see. Schoolwise Maddie's all into extracurriculars. But she struggles with her core classes—you know, math, English, history. She's a major procrastinator. Take Advanced Algebra, for example. Most people take that when they're freshmen or sophomores, right? But she waited until her senior year. And Snowcrest has a swimming requirement. But Maddie didn't want to get her hair wet during school hours, so she waited till the last minute and ended up having to take Synchronized Swimming with a bunch of freshmen."

He squints at his sandwich. "Synchronized Swimming?"

"Yeah, you know, twenty girls swimming around in circles, fluttering their hands and feet underwater like a bunch of hippo ballerinas in flowery swim caps." Okay, so I'm in that class too, but I'm not going to admit it to Derek. None of Maddie's friends would sign up with her, and she didn't want to take it all by herself, so she begged me as a last resort. In the name of sisterly solidarity I agreed. A strand of hair blows into my eyes, and I swipe it away. "So what else do you want to know about Maddie?"

He rips the page out of my notebook and folds it into quarters. "That should do for now. So tell me, how did you get started doing this? You know, matchmaking."

"It makes me happy to help people find love, and I wanted a job that made me happy." My stock answer, delivered with a wistful smile.

"That's strange."

Huh? "What do you mean?" I ask.

"Well, *most* girls are obsessed with finding boyfriends for them*selves*. In fact," he continues, picking up momentum, "they work at jobs where they can meet guys. You know, like at Hot Dog on a Stick. 'You look sexy in that enormous red-white-blue-and-yellow hat' is the best pickup line ever."

"You're really starting to scare me, Derek."

He laughs. "Not that I've ever *used* that line—"

"Yeah, right." I roll my eyes and try not to crack up.

He nods twice and then stuffs the rest of his lunch in his mouth. After swallowing and giving his mouth a quick napkin swipe, he hands me a chocolate chip cookie. "For you."

"Oh!" I smile. "Thanks."

"Thank *you*, Sasha. Thanks for helping me get a date with your sister."

"No thanks necessary, Tex. It's all in a day's work." And that's how I'm going to have to treat this. As work. Derek's PayPal payment should be deposited into my account any day now. I'm going to put a hundred and ten percent into this gig, just like all the others. Sure, Derek's adorable (sigh), and Maddie needs another guy crushing on her like the Spears sisters need more babies, but hey.

Now that I've psyched myself up, I can't wait to get these two together!

And I totally can't wait for Monday, my sixteenth birthday. I've been working so hard for six months, and I've just about paid Mrs. Woosely back for her car repair job. Now I'll be able to get my driver's license, and a new car will be sitting in the driveway with a big bow on top. I can just see it now.

I sleep like a baby the night before my sixteenth birthday, visions of Hondas, VWs, and Nissans dancing in my head. When Maddie turned sixteen, Mom took her to get her license, and when she got home, a VW Beetle was parked in the driveway with a big bow on its hood. Ever since, I've been superexcited to see what my parents would have planned for me.

When the alarm buzzes, I leap out of bed and sprint over to the window. At first I don't see anything. Then I notice there's a Vespa parked in the driveway. With a big yellow bow on the handles. *Huh?*

When what I'm seeing synchs with my brain, I about die.

Storming through the house I scream, "Where is he?"

Maddie pokes her head out of her room. "Who, Dad?"

"*Yes*, Dad. What, did he just deliver my birthday present and disappear in the night like a skinny, middle-aged Santa Claus?" Looking at Maddie with her long auburn hair and beautiful makeup-free face makes me even angrier. I could spend hours in the bathroom and still not look half as good as her right-outta-bed look. Sheesh!

She yawns and stretches out her arms. "Beats me. But he told Mom he'd take us to dinner at Papa Romano's. I guess Valerie made a cake for you and everything."

Ugh, Valerie. Her name alone makes me shudder. Oh, to be fair, Valerie's nice enough. But the instant the woman Maddie and I have always known as Dad's Boss became Dad's Girlfriend, and shortly thereafter the Reason for Our Parents' Divorce—well, let's just say those company picnics and mandatory family get-togethers have reached a whole new level of dread. And now I'm going to have to eat the cake she's making for me and pretend to be ecstatic about the freaking scooter. Wonderful.

"I just don't get it," I say, my voice all squeaky. "Did I do something to piss Dad off?" Then an even worse thought pops into my head. What if Mrs. Woosely backed out of our agreement and told him about the accident?

Maddie plants her hands on her non-existent hips and frowns. "What's got your panties in a twist, Sasha? Is it an ugly color or something? You know, you shouldn't be so picky. We're lucky to have such a generous father. Not every girl gets a car on her sweet sixteen. Take Jessica, for example. You know how her parents are totally loaded?

Well, she was almost seventeen before they bought her a car, and it's a 2002 Buick. I'm *serious*."

My mouth opens and shuts like one of those freakishly huge goldfish in the pond by Benihana. I grab Maddie's arm and drag her to my bedroom, fling open the blinds, and bang my pointer finger into the window pane.

Her big green eyes grow two sizes as she focuses on the scooter. "God, it *is* the wrong color. It'll *totally* clash with your wardrobe."

I blink, dumbfounded. "You don't think it's a little odd that he bought you a VW for your sixteenth birthday, and all I get is a freaking *scooter*?"

She shrugs one shoulder, looking a little put off. "I was just kidding, Sasha. You're not the only one in the family that can make jokes. So . . . I admit it's a little strange. But look on the bright side." She peers out the window. "It's cute, don't you think? Looks like one of those Vespas that Audrey Hepburn rode in *Roman Holiday*." She presses her lips together and says under her breath, "But I totally can't believe he chose a purple one."

"Hel-*lo*?" I whirl around and topple over onto my bed. "This is Utah, not Hawaii. What am I supposed to do when it snows?"

Maddie hugs me. "Oh, sweetie. Don't worry. I'll still give you rides. That's what big sisters are for."

Oh, great. "Um, Maddie? You can let go of me now."

I ride my new purple scooter to school that day. There's a card stuffed into the color-coordinated helmet. HAPPY BIRTHDAY TO THE SWEETEST SIXTEEN-YEAR-OLD I KNOW! is printed inside, with *I hope you like it. We had it custom-painted purple, your favorite color. Love, Dad and Val* in Dad's chicken-scratch handwriting below.

Yeah right, my fave color when I was like three and in love with Barney the Dinosaur. I cram the card into my backpack. Which, for the record, is not purple. It's *lavender*.

I can't kick the sour feeling as I try to fluff my hair in my dinky locker mirror. Am I crazy to expect a little equal treatment of sisters? Am I unreasonable to figure that since Dad bought Maddie a brand-new, sunflower-yellow VW Bug on her sweet sixteen, he'd get me something in the kingdom of transportation, phylum of vehicle, class of car, order of totally adorable?

"Happy birrrrthday to yooooooou," Yasmin sings à la Marilyn Monroe, grabbing her books out of her locker. She's wearing a halter top, a pair of low-slung jeans, and kitten heels. Her long black hair is coiled and twisted up, and her lips are painted shiny red, making her look even more exotic than usual. "Got something for ya." She slips her books into her leather satchel and then hands me a tiny box, the kind that comes from upscale jewelry stores.

"Are you proposing? Don't you think we should move in together first—you know, test the waters?" I joke.

She rolls her eyes. "As if. Just open it already."

I flip open the box and find a gold heart charm nestled in the velvety folds.

"Thanks, sweetie." I give her a quick kiss on the cheek. "I love it."

She smiles. "I knew you would." She glances down at her bangle-watch. "Well, gotta bail. I want to sit by Brian in English Lit today."

"I don't blame you." Yay!

"Oh, by the way. I like your hair better

the way you usually do it. It's all . . ." She scrunches up her nose, apparently searching for the perfect word. "Squashed."

I sigh. "The clinical term is helmet head."

She gives me a look that clearly says, *What the heck are you talking about?*

"A birthday gift from my dad."

"Soooo. He saw you banging your head against the wall again, I take it?" Her dark eyes twinkle mischievously.

"He got me a scooter. A Vespa or whatever."

"Cool! Is it fun?"

"I guess so . . . but he got me a *scooter* for my *sweet sixteen*," I say slowly, hoping it will help her catch on.

I wait for her to roll on the floor laughing, but she just stares at me. "You mean, instead of a car?"

I nod, the sour feeling rushing back into the pit of my stomach.

Yas is speechless.

"Do you want to come to my big fat American birthday dinner tonight?" I ask hopefully. If Yasmin comes, maybe Mom, Dad, and Valerie will be on their best behavior. And she could assist me in getting Maddie to notice the cute guy with the dark blue eyes sitting off in the corner of the restaurant. (Yup, I'm going to arrange for Derek to be there, enjoying an Italian meal for Maddie's viewing pleasure.) "I would've given you more notice, but I just found out myself this morning. Through the Maddie grapevine."

Yas's red lips curve downward. "I'm so sorry, Sasha, but I can't." She mumbles something about a sale at Nordstrom and then glances at her watch again. "I really need to go." Yas isn't stupid. We're not exactly up for the Fabulously Functional Family of the Year award.

"Okay, well, see you later then. Maybe we can take a spin on my new scooter . . . ?"

But Yas is already too far down the hall to hear. While a posse of bored-looking skaters coasts by, I pull out my cell phone and text Derek: *Papa Romano's at 7 tonight. I want Maddie 2 see U there, looking irresistible. Which isn't hard for U :). Just get a table and I'll take it from there. xoxo, Miss Match*

Ha! If Derek can handle our family, it's sure to win points with my sis!

Three

I casually glance around Papa Romano's, trying to see if Derek is here yet. The quaint little restaurant is totally packed. I hope he didn't already come and get turned away for not having a reservation!

Mom isn't here yet either, and the waiter is clearly set on feeding us and then shooing us out so he can turn our table as many times as possible tonight. Eventually, Dad makes the executive decision to order without Mom. Which probably wasn't the best move, because the instant her stilettos step through the double doors, I can tell she's in one of her moods. One where she shows a happily married couple a gazillion houses and they don't like a single one. Not because she cares that she spent all that time and gas money and won't be getting her six percent, but because, well, they're a happily married couple.

Mom storms across the restaurant, takes one look at Valerie, and visibly melts into the wood-planked floor. Dad flags down the waiter and supersizes his glass of wine. "Make that a bottle," he says.

"Valerie, I haven't seen you for a while," Mom says, taking her seat across from me. "You're looking especially lovely today. Have you done something different with your . . . nose?"

Valerie's hand flies to her face, and her cheeks flush the color of her raspberry lemonade.

Maddie claps her hands together. (She's always doing that. I'm afraid that one of these times she's going to automatically launch into a cheer.) "Way to go, Val! It looks *way* better. Like Ashlee Simpson's."

"Is Ashlee one of your friends at school?" Valerie asks, obviously interpreting Maddie's "compliment" as (a) an invitation to bond and (b) a chance to change the subject.

Maddie giggles, and before she has a

chance to launch into a long-winded biography that's part Wikipedia and part *Access Hollywood*, I say, "Yes, Ashlee Simpson is one of Maddie's very closest friends." Which makes Maddie giggle even more.

While the waiter performs his sommelier act, a small grin plays on Dad's lips. He takes a sip of wine before it grows into a full-fledged smile.

I do another Derek check, but he's still a no-show. Well, it won't hurt to prime Maddie for when he *does* get here. "Do you have plans later tonight, Maddie?" I ask, not waiting for her answer. "Just wondering 'cause I'm totally in the mood to watch *Failure to Launch*. You know, that movie with Sarah Jessica Parker and *Matthew McConaughey*?" I close my eyes. "Mmmm. I swear, I can get lost in that sweet southern drawl of his." When I open my eyes, I'm looking directly at Maddie.

"Isn't that the one when he's totally old, like thirty, and still living with his parents?" she asks. "What a loser."

"Uh, yeah. But isn't his voice to die for?"

She shrugs. "I guess so. But he's still a loser."

Okay, so it's obvious I'll have to try another tack. I crane my neck to see out the window, but there's no '66 Chevy pickup in the parking lot. Shoot. Where is Derek?

Then the conversation turns to the reason we're all twisting our forks in piles of noodles: my birthday. Dad asks, "Sasha, how do you like the Vespa we got you?"

What's a girl to do? Tell the truth? Pretend it's the greatest gift ever? Lie and say everything is totally cool?

"It sucks." Oops. Guess my internal filter needs to be replaced.

Everybody's eyebrows skyrocket, and Mom starts coughing, reaching desperately for her water glass.

I look Dad straight in the eyes and say, "Well, I'm sure it's fine as far as scooters go, but . . ." How do I say this without sounding like a total ingrate?

"She wanted a car." Aha. Maddie to my rescue.

Valerie places her hand on top of Dad's. She presses her lips together like I'm a nine-year-old asking about the birds and the bees. "In this day and age we believe it's best for young people to learn the value of hard work. You're sixteen now, which is a very exciting age—"

"Because I can drive now. A *car*." I take a bite of my garlic bread, crumbs exploding all over the red-and-white-checked table-cloth.

Valerie sits up straighter, staring me down with her beady little eyes. "Because you can get a job, Sasha. And earn the money to buy a car for yourself. Just think how much more that car will mean to you when you've *earned* it."

Maddie nods. "True story. When I made cheerleader freshman year, it really meant a lot to me, 'cause I did it all by myself. Instead of having my father, who happens to be the *governor*, make a phone call to the athletic department. Not that I'm naming names." She mouths "Kennedy" to me across the table.

I bite the inside of my cheek, realizing that Maddie isn't the problem. It's not her fault she's so clueless. It's not *her* fault she was born unbelievably beautiful and thin and perfect and gets *everything* she freaking wants out of life, while I get the few hand-me-downs that I can stuff myself into, rides in her VW when it's snowing, and (lest we forget!) a Barney the Dinosaur scooter.

Mom speaks up. "Richard, don't you think that since you gave Maddie a car when *she* turned sixteen, it would only be fair to buy one for Sasha?"

I cross my arms on the table, eyeing Dad. Again, Val's hand finds its way onto his. Funny, but while Valerie seems to be looking better and better—even glowing— Dad appears wilted and stressed out. He's looking in every direction except my eyes. Dad loosens his tie a notch, seemingly buying time. "To be honest, I'm not so sure we didn't make a mistake, Sue."

I glance at my sister through the corner of my eye, but she's just munching her salad merrily, either (a) unfazed by Dad's words, (b) unhearing of Dad's words, or (and I lay my money on this one) (c) uncomprehending of Dad's words.

Mom shifts her jaw from side to side, exclamation marks in her eyes.

Looks like Dad's got a rod up the back of his shirt. "Listen, Sue. I realize we don't see eye to eye on everything, but Sasha is perfectly capable of earning enough money to buy a car. It wouldn't hurt her to have an after-school job, since she's not cheerleading like Maddie, or playing sports . . ."

A horrible thought infiltrates my mind and brings goose bumps to my skin. Does Dad love Maddie more than me? Is she the Favorite Daughter and I'm just a black sheep, a rotten apple on the Finnegan family tree?

Before I can completely indulge my insecurities, Dad meets my eyes. "I love you, Sasha. But times are changing. These days, you can't get a college scholarship on good grades alone. Part-time jobs really give you a step up." He starts blathering on about motivation and whatnot, mostly for Mom's benefit, and I politely tune out. Except now Valerie is vying for my attention and starts a little tête-à-tête on the sidelines. Lucky me.

"You'll be saving money on gas, Sasha. Vespas are better for the environment," Valerie declares, digging into her pasta.

"Won't I have to get a whole different kind of license to drive it?" I ask, tagging on a weak, "Legally?" when I realize that I very well might have driven it illegally to school today.

"Eventually, you will have to get your motorcycle license, but I hear the classes are a lot of fun. Plus, you might meet a handsome young man in yours." She takes a bite and chews thoroughly before swallowing. "For now you just have to take a written exam, which will get you a temporary permit that's good for six whole months. Then you can show it to all your friends, take them on spins. I'm sure they'll all be envious."

Okay, this conversation has gone far enough. I smile at Valerie as if she's just hit a home run—that my friends being jealous is my sole goal in life—and shift my attention back to my parents. Whose discussion can *not* be any worse than Valerie's and mine.

Mom says, "I'm not sure, Richard." She hasn't touched the vegetarian lasagna Dad ordered for her. "I really think you're being unfair. And with the real-estate market so slow, I can't even afford to buy her a Yugo."

"I don't think they make those anymore, Susan," Valerie says softly.

Mom shoots her a vicious *stay out of it, you nasty homewrecker* glare.

Dad fidgets and blows out a puff of air. "Okay, maybe we can compromise, then."

"They don't call you the king of compromise for nothing," Mom mumbles, poking her fork in the lasagna and leaving it there.

Dad takes a hefty swig of his wine. "If

Sasha gets a job and works hard, I'll match whatever she earns." He pats his mouth with his napkin and then grins benevolently. What, does he expect me to cry for joy or give him a standing ovation or something?

I feel like I'm going to explode. Which would be way gross, 'cause I've been stuffing myself with spaghetti for about thirty minutes. I shove my chair back, bolt upright, and stomp to the ladies' room. I hear Mom say, "Now look what you've done," probably to Dad. Unless Maddie spilled her Diet Coke all over the table, which is entirely possible.

When I come back and plunk down in my chair, all I get is crickets. I scarf my piece of homemade chocolate birthday cake, which is admittedly to-die-for delicious. How did Val know I'm a chocoholic? Well, it's the least Val could do for stealing away our father and sucking all the sense out of his brain.

To make matters worse, Derek never shows up. There's nothing more frustrating than a client who doesn't give one hundred percent. Especially when there's less than a month to work with. I can hand him the bat and help predict the pitch, but he's gonna have to step up to the plate!

After first-period American Government, I run into the ladies' room to check my appearance. Luckily, I haven't busted out of my jeans yet. You never know, what with all that chocolate cake I ate last night. I fluff my ponytail—the only hairstyle that seems to work after my hair's been stuffed in a helmet—and daub on the lipstick Maddie gave me. (She thought her new first-day-of-school color looked better on me.) Next stop: Chem Lab.

Hurrying toward room 116 I yank my emergency brake when I see Kevin McGregor, a senior whose face is splashed across virtually every page of Snowcrest High's yearbook. He's leaning against Maddie's locker. Which is no big deal. Except that he's leaning in to Maddie, whispering something in her ear that has her giggling like a loon on nitrous oxide.

"Hi, Maddie!" I say, all chipper. "Are you heading this way?" I nod in the direction from which I just came. Thing is, I know very well that her next "class" is in the attendance office. I've memorized her school schedule as part of Derek's matchmaking gig. Not waiting for her to answer, I grab her elbow and snatch her away from the two-hundred-pound wide receiver. "Great, I'll walk with you! We'd better hurry. The bell's going to ring any second, and you don't want to be late."

As I whisk her away, she waves at Kevin, and he just kind of stands there, watching her with a dopey expression on his face. I escort my sister to the office, and as soon as she passes through the door, I flat-out run to Chemistry Lab.

I get to class a mere twenty seconds before the bell, all breathless. Derek swaggers over to me and says in that sweet Southern drawl, "Wanna pair up with the new kid?"

"Er . . ."

"Cool! Looks like everyone else already has partners."

He sits down beside me, and I get a whiff of his sexy cologne. Oh, good, he took my tip. It's just a hint, enough to notice, but not so much it's overwhelming. Maddie's going to love it when they have their tutor session tomorrow afternoon.

He hands me the lab sheet and spreads out his binder. "Choose a lab partner" is printed on the blackboard, and Mr. Foley diligently scrawls "How Bonding Affects Acidity."

Just as Mr. Foley instructs us to begin, my sister walks in. Her red and black cheerleader skirt swishes around her long, spray-on-tan thighs. I hear my new lab partner gasp. He's spellbound, just like every other guy in the room. She sashays over to the blackboard and hands Mr. Foley a pink piece of paper.

Mr. Foley twitches his bushy gray mustache as he scans the note. "Thank you, young lady," he says, adding the paper to the clutter on his desk.

She nods in her official attendance-office-helper way and turns to leave. Right before her red and black K-Swisses reach the door, she catches my eye. "Hey, Sasha! Tell Mom I won't be home for dinner, okay?"

Where's she going to be? I wonder. Normally, I wouldn't care. But now that she's the object of my client's affection, I've got to keep tabs on her. "No problem."

Once Maddie is out of sight, Mr. Foley starts marching up and down between the tables, making sure we're all on the right track.

"Where were you last night?" I ask my new lab partner after Mr. Foley passes by.

Derek bites his lower lip for a split second. "Oh, well, my dad was grilling steaks and . . ."

I shake my head, giving him my *tut-tut* face. "You have to work with me, Derek. I can't do my job if you don't show up. It's important that you two are in the same picture as often as possible. She can't fall for you if you aren't ever around."

"Right. Sorry. Next time I'll just eat dinner twice." He fixes his dark blue eyes on me like he's just told a hilarious joke and he's waiting for me to crack up. Finally realizing that this is no laughing matter, he scratches the back of his neck and says, "I know you're trying really hard to fix me up, and I promise from here on out I'll do my part." He holds four fingers up. "Scout's honor."

I take his hand and lower his pinky. "There." Then I cave in and let a smile break through.

Mr. Foley clears his throat, which makes his mustache wiggle. How long has he been standing there? I glance down at the lab instruction sheet and run my finger down the page, pretending to be all into it.

When the coast is clear of snoopy teachers, Derek whispers, "Hey, Sasha?" He carefully fills the buret with the 0.250 M NaOH.

"Mmm?" I jot down the buret reading on the specified line and grab the Erlenmeyer flask for the next step. Man, Derek and I definitely work well together. "I have some good news, and I think it'll more than make up for me messing up last night with the restaurant and everything. I'm still making adjustments to my school schedule, so I figured, why not take a class with Maddie, you know, so we can get to know each other better? See how you and me are getting to know each other, being in this class together? And like you said, it's hard for a girl to fall for someone if he's never around."

I beam at him. "That's fantastic, Derek. Good thinking!"

He stoops over and unzips the front pocket of his Burton backpack. "I'm taking Synchronized Swimming," he says, dangling a pair of neon-green goggles before my eyes.

The flask falls, glass shattering on the floor. Twenty-three heads turn and forty-six eyes zero in on me. Oh, God. He did *not* just say he's taking Synchronized Swimming.

"Oops!" is all I can think of to say.

"It's okay," Derek says, making a beeline for the cleanup closet.

Oh, but it's *not* okay. The only saving grace of being in Synchronized Swimming is that there are no guys in it whatsoever. Derek can *not* see me in my nose clip and überugly Speedo one-piece. This is the worst news ever!

After taking the written exam so I'm a legal Vespa rider (which I have to admit wasn't a big deal after all), I wander into the kitchen in pursuit of an after-school snack. Since I didn't eat lunch, I'm totally starved. With Mom working so late, and with Maddie's bustling social life, we never eat dinner before seven, or sometimes even eight.

Speaking of Maddie, I've got to figure out where the heck she is. Or, more importantly, *who* the heck she's *with*. That Kevin McGregor dude has been loitering around her lately, and I've got to make sure he doesn't ask Maddie to the homecoming dance. I call her cell.

"Hey, Sasha. What's up?" she says.

"Hi. Um, just calling to see what you're doing."

"Oh, not much. Just downloading a few songs over at Kevin's. Ever heard of Seven's Sake? They're the coolest band ever! They totally sound like Depeche Mode."

Oh no. This is not good. Must think fast. "I was thinking maybe you should come home," I say, rummaging through my mind for a compelling reason. "Mom's all depressed, and I was going to make a really good dinner to try and lift her spirits. So what do you say?"

"That woman's always depressed."

"It's probably because her oldest daughter is never home anymore. She misses you, Maddie."

After a brief pause Maddie says, "You're right. Okay, I'll be there."

As I hang up the phone, it's clear I've got to find out more about Kevin and Maddie's relationship. I hope it's not too late.

"Hi, honey," Mom says, coming into the kitchen. I just sent an e-mail to Hunter, giving him directions and even attaching a kick-butt diagram of how to stuff folded paper in the doorjamb of Anna's locker for Operation Paper Stick. I'm totally excited to hear how it goes!

Mom is a classic beauty, an older version of Maddie. However, when she's tired, like today, she's all dark under-eye circles and sunken cheeks. At the risk of sounding mean, I'm glad she looks so beat, 'cause Maddie's psyched about saving Mom from her "depression."

"Wow, something sure smells good," Mom says wistfully.

"Halibut Olympia. I thought I'd make something special." Mom's a vegetarian for the most part, but she sometimes splurges on fish.

She peeks into the oven and smiles. "Sasha, you're a gem."

Ten minutes later the stench of burnt potatoes fills the air. Great. Mom, Maddie, and I take our seats at the kitchen table and dig into the halibut, spinach salad (sans bacon), and the nonblackened portion of roasted potatoes. From time to time Mom's gaze flits to the empty seat at the end of the table, where Dad used to sit.

"Are you doing better in algebra?" Mom asks Maddie, asking the sort of question Dad would ask if he were here.

"Let's not talk about something so depressing," Maddie says with her mouth full. "Life's too short to worry about little things like math and *divorce*."

Mom purses her lips together and says nothing. Her cell phone rings, and she excuses herself to answer it. That's the thing about being a real-estate agent. Calls equal money, and we'd have to be in the hospital or something for her not to answer.

I dissect a potato with my fork and then look up at my sister. "I wasn't going to mention this, 'cause I know it's none of my business. But I'd feel horrible if I kept it a secret and you had to give up everything you've worked so hard on all these years."

"What are you talking about?" Maddie asks, poking at her salad.

"It's algebra. I was in the math office this morning, you know, turning in some extra credit, and I happened to see a list on Ms. Brown's desk. Looks like your name is on the Ineligible Athletes list."

She gasps, showing me a mouthful of chewed-up spinach. "Cheerleading?"

"I guess Snowcrest assumes that cheerleading is athletic. It's a pretty loose definition, but . . ."

She gives me the evil eye, but I know she knows I'm just razzing her. She takes cheerleading very seriously, and there's no way I could ever do those stunts she does without breaking my neck. Then Maddie shakes her head, her supershiny hair swishing across her shoulders. "I can't get kicked off the team. It's my *life*."

"I know, I know." I pat her back, which is probably overdoing it, but hey, I didn't take drama last semester for nothin'.

"What am I going to do?" she asks, her green eyes pleading.

I shrug. "Beats me. I mean, you already waited as long as you could to take it. And even though not being a cheerleader would be tragic, what if you don't graduate?"

Another gasp, another spinach peep show. "I've got to do something! I just totally don't get algebra." Her eyes suddenly brighten. "*You* could teach me, Sasha. You're so good at mathy stuff."

I bite my lower lip. "Actually, I know this guy who's an algebra genius." I frown and then say, "Oh, wait. Never mind."

She drops her fork with a clank. "What is it?"

"Well," I say, walking over to the fridge for another Diet Coke, "he's so amazing at tutoring that he's all booked up."

"He can't fit one more person in?"

"I'm afraid not."

She's standing up now, her voice squeaky in desperation. "Call him, Sasha! Call him and *beg*. You'll do that for me, won't you? You're my sister!"

"Well . . . I guess it wouldn't hurt. Maybe he had a cancellation or something."

"That would be *so* cool!" She claps her hands together as if she's about to start a cheer. Good God.

I pick up the cordless phone and, without powering it on, punch the buttons. Then I pretend to be talking to Derek. "Hi, Derek. It's me, Sasha. . . . I'm good, how about you? . . . Great. Well, I know this sounds weird and all, but I need to ask you a favor. . . . Okay, here goes. My sister—you don't know her but she's really cool—she needs someone to help her with algebra. Naturally, I thought of you. . . . I know, and I told her that. But she's totally desperate. Snowcrest might confiscate her pompoms if she doesn't get her grade up to a C. . . . Oh? Really? . . . Let me ask."

I clamp my hand over the receiver and look up at Maddie. She's watching me with as much interest as she watches old Audrey

Hepburn movies. "He says he can fit you in at four o'clock Wednesday afternoon."

She raises her eyebrows for an instant and then lowers them disappointedly. "Tomorrow? Shoot. I was going to the Gateway with Kevin. He needs to find a birthday present for his evil stepsister."

I say, "Oh," and then put the phone to my ear again. "Sorry, but she's got important plans. Thanks any—"

"Wait! Uh, okay. I'll do it. Kevin can wait."

I shrug and try not to smile. "Derek? You still there? . . . She'll meet you in the library by the biographies. . . . Cool. See ya around." I hook the phone on its cradle, and Maddie runs over and gives me a hug.

"You're the best, Sasha. Thank you thank you thank you!"

She'll really be thanking me when she sees how cute her new tutor is.

Four

It's 4:05 Wednesday afternoon. Derek is at his station, rigid in his chair, acting like he's absorbed in a geography textbook. I whistle to get his attention and give him the thumbs-up. He nods and then resumes his not-so-casual waiting act.

I slip the atlas back in its slot and sneeze when some dust flies into my nostrils. A lively group of sophomores files out of the library with their stacks of borrowed loot.

Okay. So it's 4:10 p.m., and there's still no sign of Maddie. I run over to Derek and tell him, "I'll go to the gym and see if she's still there."

He smiles at me, dimple and all. "All right."

The gym is populated with the women's volleyball team and not cheerleaders. Shoot. I sink onto a bleacher and call Maddie's cell. "Hello?" she says in her pink bubblegum voice. Hip-hop blares in the background.

"Maddie! Where are you?"

She giggles. "Headin' over to the Gateway. Why?"

"What about your algebra tutor?"

"Oh no! I totally spaced that." A pause. "I'm really not that far. I can come back. Tell him to wait up, 'kay?"

"Okay." I slide my phone shut, feeling deflated. How could Maddie have forgotten? I should've picked her up after cheerleading practice and physically dragged her to the library. My bad.

What am I supposed to tell Derek? To wait even longer and cross his fingers that she makes it at all? Or should we just call it a day, and start from square one tomorrow?

Picturing him sitting in the library, so hopeful and nervous, I'm fed up with my sister. I can't let her get away with this—forgetting all about their meeting and making him wait so long for her to show. Sure, she thought it was just to get some help with her math. To him, however, it was so much more.

I jog back to the library and accidentally bump into a cart of books. Bending down to pick up the tomes that toppled off, I find myself face-to-toe with the librarian's blue suede pumps. "Sasha, so nice to see you!" she says in her petal-soft voice. "Can I help you find anything?"

"Uh, no thanks," I say, rising. "I'm just looking for someone . . ."

Mrs. Leonard follows my gaze across the library to where Derek is sitting, surfing the Internet or something. Then he swivels to look out the window, resting his chin on his hand. I can't be sure from this distance, but he seems a little sad.

"Looks like you found him," Mrs. Leonard says, interrupting my formulation of Plan B.

She gives me this *go get 'im, tiger* smile and nods her head in Derek's direction. I feel my face heat up, even though she's got it all wrong. I hand her the books and make a beeline over to him.

I clear my throat, praying my voice won't come out all croaky. "Derek? I'm terribly sorry, but something came up and Maddie can't meet you today. She wants to know if she can have a rain check. How about tomor-row, same time?"

He powers down the computer and scoots out his chair with an earsplitting screech. "I guess that'll work," he says. He grins at me, but I can tell he's more than a little bit disappointed.

"Is everything okay?" I ask, sitting beside him.

He stares down at his hand, which is absently tracing the initials that some loser carved into the table like a freaking cave-man. "It's not me, is it? Did she take one look at me and scram?"

I snort-laugh. My sister might not be the brightest lipstick at the MAC counter, but I'm sure she wouldn't have any difficulty gazing across the table at Derek. "No! It's just that she . . ." I'm tempted to tell him the truth, that she totally forgot their meet-ing. That she's ditzy like that. But I need to hold her in the best possible light. So I say, "Something came up; that's all. Really."

Riding home on my purple scooter, I feel lousy about having lied to Derek. But I don't want Maddie to think she can just jerk him around. Besides, I don't want Derek to come off as the pathetic, desperate type. So I tell myself I'm lying for the greater good, and by the time I'm home, I feel much better.

After grabbing some pretzels, I go up to my room and swap my jeans for a pair of comfy sweats. I boot up my laptop and then type:

Subj: Assignment
Date: Sept. 15, 5:06 PM Mountain Standard Time
From: MissMatch@MissMatch4Hire.com
To: PrincessYasmin@kmail.com

Hey Yas,

Do you think you can dig up some dirt on Kevin McGregor?

xoxo
Sasha

Maddie storms into my room, cheeks flushed. "So I made Kevin speed the whole way back to school, and when I got there, the only ones in the library were Mrs. Leonard and the Thompson triplets." She plops onto my bed and kicks off her K-Swisses. I still can't believe Maddie forgot all about her meeting with Derek. *I* sure as heck wouldn't have forgotten.

I hit send and close my laptop. "I'm sorry, Maddie. I told him you were on your way, but by the time I pushed through all the girls who were swarming him, he said he couldn't wait any longer." Yep, the ol' Scarlett O'Hara approach to getting a crush's attention: Surround oneself with members of the opposite sex and act utterly irresistible. Knowing my sis and (a) her competitive spirit and (b) her obsession with what the Snowcrest High student body thinks of her, she'll be dying to meet him and ante up, so to speak. "I think I saw him leave with Kennedy."

"Kennedy Henderson?" Maddie asks. Kennedy is the cheerleading captain, and though they're supposedly friends, I know Maddie secretly wishes the Hendersons would move to Kansas so she'd have less competition for . . . well, everything. The most pressing contest, naturally, being homecoming queen. But Kennedy's dad is the governor, so it looks like their family is here to stay—at least until his term is over.

"Yeah, I think it was her. I can't be sure, though. She had really pretty hair and dressed way cute."

Maddie sighs. "That definitely sounds like Kennedy." She runs her fingers over the books in my bookcase. She tips *Emma* forward, taps it a couple of times, then slides it back into place, between *Pride and Prejudice* and *The Importance of Being Earnest*. "I really wanted some help on my homework. I totally don't get it."

"I'll help you today. And maybe Derek can help you tomorrow. How does four o'clock sound?"

"Super!"

Scratch Plan B. It's time for Plan C. Basically, Maddie will meet her secret admirer in Synch Swimming first, and then have her tutoring session after school. It's going to work like a charm!

But wait. I'm so not looking forward to doing the whole hippo-ballerina act in front of Derek tomorrow. Why did he have to sign up for Synchronized Swimming, anyway?

On Thursday morning in the women's locker room, I get the news straight from the horse's mouth. Well, from *Yasmin's* mouth, but it might as well be the horse's. "Kevin McGregor is going to ask your sister to homecoming. *Today*."

I gasp. "How do you know?"

"I overheard a bunch of football players in the hall. They were talking about cool ways to ask chicks to the dance." She slides her superslim body into her pants.

"So can you narrow it down a little for me? Did he say exactly when he was going to ask her, or how?" Maybe I can make an interception or sabotage it somehow. Whatever I do, I've got to buy some time so Derek can ask her first. I peel off my hoodie, wishing for the body beneath to have miraculously toned and slimmed to something I wouldn't mind showing off in a swimming suit. No such luck.

"I'm not sure. He didn't say."

"So that's it? No . . . dirt?"

"He's clean, Sasha."

"Shoot."

"Can you hand me that boot?" she asks.

I grab her black knee-high boot off the bench and pass it to her, then watch her button up her cropped jacked and flip her hair over the collar. Every strand falls beautifully in place. I gather my hair in a messy bun and snap an elastic band around it. After I say good-bye to Yas, I suck in a deep breath. Though I'm dreading Derek being in Synch

Swimming, at least I'll get to warn him about his clear and present competition. And with Maddie safe within the confines of the swimming pool, Kevin won't have a chance to ask her yet.

Speaking of Maddie, where is she? Shouldn't she be changing into her swimming suit now?

When I walk past the full-length mirror by the toilets, I tell myself not to look. But curiosity gets the better of me, and I take a cursory peek at my reflection. Ugh. My breasts are too small, my hips are too big, my stomach is lumpy, and my thighs look like tree trunks. Well, unless there's a fairy godmother or genie stashed in one of these stalls, I'm going to have to make do with what I've got. I pull my shoulders back and suck in my stomach—enough to engage my ab muscles, but not so much I look like I'm trying. Then I wrap my towel around my body and head out to the pool, my flip-flops slapping against my heels.

The humid, chlorine-scented air greets me, along with Coach White, Snowcrest High's bespectacled and buff swimming coach. "I hope Maddie feels better soon," Coach says all sympathetically. Her high-pitched voice echoes all around the pool area.

"Oh?" I'm about to ask what ails Maddie, knowing full and well that she's just ditching, but I think better of it. You know, in case it's something like tonsillitis or a brain tumor—something a sister should definitely know about. "That's kind of you to say, Coach." I smile at her and make my squeaky ascent onto the bleachers with the rest of the class. The rest of the class minus one Derek Urban and one Maddie Finnegan, that is. Too bad they're not ditching together, doing something totally romantic.

Then a terrible (yet much more realistic) thought crosses my mind, completely wrecking the lovey-dovey scene I was just imagining. What if Maddie is skipping class to hang out with Kevin? What if he is asking her to homecoming *right this very second*?

My stomach goes all knotty, which only gets worse when I spot Derek. He swaggers over to Coach White, his tan, muscular body half naked. I promptly avert my eyes, but then I realize the entire class is ogling him. I'm not sure if it's because (a) he's lookin' oh-so-hot in those surfer shorts or (b) he's the only nonfemale to ever set foot into the pool area for this particular class.

Sara and Trinity, who are flanking me, give Derek bashful smiles and immediately straighten their postures. Hmm. Maybe I won't have to make up any more stories about girls batting their eyelashes at the handsome new guy. You know, to help ratchet up Maddie's interest in him.

Derek takes a quick break from whatever he's chatting about with Coach and gives me a confused look followed by a little wave. I smile back and shrug. When the other girls whip around to look at me, I can feel my face turning red. "Sasha, do you know him?" Trinity stage-whispers.

"He's in my chemistry class."

"He's going to be in Synch Swimming?" she asks.

I give her a half smile, just now realizing that I've been biting my lower lip. "Looks like it." The girls begin talking and gesturing animatedly (as freshmen are prone to do) about this newest development.

Coach blows her whistle, startling everybody into abrupt silence. "All right, ladies. Er, I mean, *people*," she amends, shooting Derek an apologetic look. "It's time to get warmed up. We've already wasted five minutes, so get to it. Take your places and start with some stretches."

The girls shed their towels and flip-flops on the bleachers and hightail it to the area at the west end of the pool. I hurry to secure a spot in the back row, hoping no one says anything about my being the only one who's still got a towel wrapped around her waist.

Derek, the object of much rubbernecking, stands beside me. He reaches up his arms. Next he clasps his hands behind his head, making his biceps *boing* out quite . . . well, quite nicely, I suppose. "Sasha, why didn't you tell me you were in this class?" he whispers, as Coach counts down the arm/back stretch we're all supposed to be holding right now.

"I didn't want to scare you off."

"Ahh. Well, you've obviously never seen my synchronized-swimming moves." He chuckles, and some of the girls turn to look at him. He clears his throat and performs the next stretch. "*I've* never even seen my synchronized-swimming moves, come to think of it."

"Okay, class, ten laps. Go!" Coach claps and the girls obey like a pack of golden retrievers.

Okay, here goes. The shedding of the protective towel. Now Derek will know what I meant by not wanting to scare him off.

Snap out of it, Sasha. He's only here 'cause he's got a thing for Maddie. He couldn't care less if I had the body of what's-her-face who's on the cover of *Sports Illustrated*'s swimsuit issue. I whip off the towel and dive into the chilly water. Ten laps later everyone's lined up along the wall in the deep end, huffing and puffing.

Well, everyone except Derek. He's doing an impressive butterfly in the far lane. How'd he know Coach's favorite stroke? He'll probably get extra credit. We all watch in virtual silence until he pulls himself out of the water, his broad chest undulating as he catches his breath.

"Better be careful, or she's going to recruit you for the swim team," I whisper to him while Coach goes over the day's agenda. I can't help but notice how sexy his hair looks when it's dripping wet. Okay, so it's not just his hair.

The class streams by in a blur. How can I concentrate on eggbeaters and paddle sculls when Kevin might be asking Maddie to homecoming at any minute? I still have to warn Derek. When it's time to hit the showers, I wrap my towel around me burrito-style and run after Derek, who's hotfooting it to the men's locker room. "Derek! Wait up!"

He smiles kind of sheepishly. What, is he embarrassed or something? "What?" I ask.

"I didn't think to bring a towel. I know, my IQ just took a major nosedive. Bet you're glad you hooked up with me."

What? Freshmen girl heads turn. Now it's my turn to look embarrassed.

He notices that we have an audience and fiddles with his goggles. "Er, to be chemistry lab partners," he stammers.

"Right, of course. Well, we'll see what kind of grade we get and I'll tell you then," I say, loud enough for all the eavesdroppers to hear. Then, more quietly, "I have an extra towel in my locker. Hang on a sec and I'll grab it."

He smiles. "Thanks, Sasha."

I take my time fetching the towel— which has a big yellow Funshine Bear on it, but at least it's freshly washed—so I can have him all to myself. Once the locker room fills with wet, chattery chicks, I head back out to the pool. "Here ya go," I say, handing the towel to Derek.

He rubs it through his hair and then shakes his head like he's got water in his ears. "Man, that was quite the workout. You girls are tough!"

I laugh. "Well, it's too bad Maddie wasn't here. But you'll get to meet her after school. So that's cool . . ." Oh! Wait a minute. I can't tell Derek that Kevin's hot on Maddie's trail when he hasn't officially met her yet. Derek might panic and ask her to the dance right away. Maddie would think he was totally whacked, and she'd find a nice way to let him down easy. His chances with her would be forever ruined! I can't let that happen. Best to just play it cool until they meet. I hope they hit it off!

Five

The rest of the day I stake out Maddie's
locker, but I don't catch Kevin in the act.
Which is good, 'cause it's almost time for
Maddie's Algebra Tutorial: Take Two.

Maddie spots me in the hallway and says,
"Hey, sweetie."

We stand by her locker for a few minutes, people watching. I figure it's best to
just stay with her so she doesn't get sidetracked this time. I check my watch. Still a
few more minutes till she needs to head to
the library.

"So how was Synch Swimming?" she
asks, rummaging in her locker.

"Where were you, by the way?" I'm sure
it has something to do with hanging out

with her friends, or worse, Kevin. I'm not so sure I want to hear the answer.

"I was studying."

"Really?" Shoot. That just slipped out. I don't want to piss Maddie off. After all, she needs to be in the best mood possible when she meets Derek for the first time.

She whips around to face me and snarls, "This might come as a surprise to you, Sasha, but I really do want to get good grades. And it's more than just staying on the cheerleading squad." She slams her locker shut. "I want to prove to myself that I'm smart. Like you."

"But you *are* smart, Maddie," I say, feeling simultaneously lousy for having doubted her integrity and relieved that she wasn't ditching to be with Kevin. "You just need a little help now and then, that's all."

Waving her algebra book in my face, she says, "And I'm getting it."

"Yes, you are. Well, I'd better let you go get that help. Have fun!" I point her in the right direction and smooth a flyaway on the top of her head. Once I've sent her off, I follow her down the hall, all quiet so she won't notice me.

When I get to the library, I peep in

to make sure she finds Derek. She walks straight over to him. Aw, how sweet. Looks like he dressed up a little more than usual. He's sporting a maroon polo and chinos and his hair looks freshly combed. I bet he smells wonderful.

I sneak in closer and hide behind the biography shelf, listening in on their conversation. It's Miss Match's responsibility to make sure this meeting goes as smoothly as possible.

Maddie is the first to speak. "Thanks for helping me . . ." She gives him that void *what the heck is your name* look.

"Derek. It's my pleasure, Maddie." He stands and holds out his hand.

She looks at him like he's crazy. Come on, Maddie. Work with him . . .

She takes his hand and shakes it, outing her dazzling smile. "My sister says you're the best algebra tutor ever."

He waits for her to sit and then follows suit. "Well, I don't know about that . . ."

Ah, modesty. Good goin', Derek.

"I haven't seen you around."

"My family just moved to Utah."

"Oh? Where are you from? Australia or somewhere?"

"Australia?"

Australia?

"You've got an accent."

It takes every ounce of self-control for me not to laugh out loud.

"Actually, I'm from Paris."

"Oooooh! Well, that explains it. How exciting!"

"Er, yeah."

"Are you looking for something in particular, Sasha?" I about jump out of my skin when Mrs. Leonard accosts me. I look up at her and smile, acting like I'm really into these biographies and not eavesdropping in the least.

"Nope, I'm doing just fine down here; thanks for your help," I whisper ever so quietly, sending a telepathic *Go away before you blow my cover!* message to the overly attentive librarian. I don't move a muscle, scared Derek or Maddie will discover me crouching behind the shelf.

Mrs. Leonard arches an eyebrow at the Donald Trump book in my hand and peers over at Derek and Maddie. "I see."

Once she finally leaves me in peace, I venture a quick peek through the books. They're both leaning over Maddie's math assignment, oblivious to the spy on the other side of the bookshelf. Whew. Close call! Convinced the two potential lovebirds have gotten off to a good start, I leave to track Kevin down and run a little interference.

When I catch up with the football players out on the field, it sounds like Coach Cunningham is wrapping up practice. "And no drinking this weekend, guys. I need everyone to be in tip-top shape if we're going to clobber Harrison for the big homecoming game."

The players sound off their grunts and howls and then stampede toward the locker room. I stay put under the bleachers for a few beats before trailing Kevin and his posse.

"Dude, did I tell you guys Kennedy said yes?" a junior called Bart says.

"To homecoming?" Kevin asks.

Another guy jumps in. "What did ya do? Threaten to book all her hairstylist's appointments from now till the big day unless she said yes to you?" They laugh and slap Bart on the back. I never knew Kennedy's hair was a hot topic in the male circle as well as the female. Seriously, that girl's locks are unreal. And she knows it.

"So did you ask Maddie to the dance?"

one of the guys asks Kevin. I scurry to catch up. I don't want to miss any important info.

"Not yet. But I'm all set to do it. She's getting tutored by some brainiac in the library right now. I'll just meet her at her locker when she's done."

"Cool."

Not cool. Okay, this is it. I've got to be on my toes. As the boys file into the locker room, I pull out my cell and dial Yasmin.

"Hey, girl, what's up?" she answers.

"Can you meet me at school? I'll be at Maddie's locker."

"You betcha. I'm just at Subway. See you in five."

I race to the library and sneak a quick look at my subjects. They're still sitting side by side, bent over Maddie's textbook. If I didn't know better, I'd think they were whispering sweet nothings to each other. It won't be long, if everything goes as planned. But anyhow it doesn't look like they're in any hurry to wrap up this lesson. Relieved, I jog back to Maddie's locker, where Yasmin is waiting. "Maddie's in the library," I tell her. "Stake out the door and call me when she's heading this way."

"Gotcha. I'll just hang out by our lockers.

Mine already needs to be cleaned out." And with that, my friend slips into Miss Match sidekick mode.

I hear guys laughing and poke my head around the corner. It's Kevin and a couple of his buddies. They're coming! I flip open my notebook, slither down to a sitting position, and pretend to be writing. It's my signature *I'm minding my own business* routine.

"You're such a dork, dude," one of the guys says. "That has got to be the lamest thing I've ever heard of. Toilet paper? Dude, get real." The jocks smell freshly showered, and when I steal a quick peek, I see they're wearing coordinated shorts and baseball caps.

"Yeah, well, she's gonna love it." Sounds like Kevin. "It's *creative*. Flowers and balloons are totally overdone."

"Say whatever you want, but asking a girl with a roll of ass-wipe is just *wrong*."

My cell phone rings. It's Yasmin, undoubtedly calling to give me an update on Maddie and Derek. Maybe they've wrapped up and Maddie's heading to her locker this very minute! Before I have a chance to answer, however, three heads pop around the corner.

"What are you doing here?" Bart asks.

"Hello, guys!" I say, pleasantly enough. "Don't mind me. I'm just writing in my journal." I waggle my pen in the air. "You know, for English class."

Kevin looks at me all weird. He's holding a roll of Charmin. *If you gotta go, go with Kevin* is scrawled on it with a thick black Sharpie. Oh my God! I can't keep it in another nanosecond. I let out this horrendous snort-laugh.

"Aren't you going to answer that?" he asks. Right. My phone is definitely still ringing. "Hey, aren't you Maddie's little sister?"

I rise and stuff my notebook into my backpack. Finally, the phone shuts up. Then I hear Yasmin's kitten heels clicking on the floor. Is she running? Yikes! Maddie's got to be close.

Fake sneezing, I snatch the toilet paper out of Kevin's hands. "Oh, crap! I must be allergic—*Aaa-choo!*—to your aftershave"—I start unrolling the paper like crazy and blow my nose—"or your jock-itch powder or something." I unroll even more and blow away, hoping the snotty noises I'm making with my mouth sound convincing. After I've used up half the roll, I toss the enormous wad in the trash can and hand the remainder of the TP back to Kevin.

He's staring at me, agog. His friends are rolling.

"Wow," I say, after I catch my breath. "That was crazy. Thank you so much for offering me your paper."

Maddie waves good-bye to Derek, and he veers toward the student parking lot. She's coming straight for us, smiling widely. Her lesson must've gone well. Yay!

But I don't have time to celebrate. I've got to keep Kevin from popping the question.

"Oh, hey guys," Maddie singsongs, cradling her algebra book. When she notices me, she looks around suspiciously. "Hey, sis. What are you still doing here?"

"Oh. Um, I had a little homework to finish."

She scrunches her nose. "But can't you do it, you know, at *home*?"

"Right. Well, you know me. The big geek. Can't get enough of this fluorescent lit prison."

She giggles and pats me on the head like a doggie. I smile obediently.

Yas is waving at me from down the hall. When no one is watching, I give her the thumbs-up. The Miss Match sidekick takes off, another job well done and majorly appreciated.

However, my job here isn't done. Not yet.

"And what are you guys doing at my locker?" Maddie asks the guys, twirling her hair. "Don't you have somewhere important to be?" She pokes Kevin's arm playfully. "Don't tell me you guys were going to TP my locker! That's so last year."

Kevin gives his friends a covert nudge. "Well, we're outta here," Bart says. The other guys grunt something and then bail.

This is getting dangerously close to an opportune moment for Kevin. The way I figure it, the only thing that's stopping him from asking Maddie to the dance right this very moment is . . . me! And I'm not going anywhere, not without my sister.

Kevin tosses the toilet paper into the trash can. "So, Maddie. What's up this weekend? Any parties?"

Maddie squints at me. "Sasha?"

"Hmm?"

"Did you need something?"

"Oh!" *Think fast, Miss Match.* "Well, actually . . . yes. My, uh . . . Vespa won't start up. Can I get a ride home?"

"Sure. I'll just meet you outside." Oh, man. This isn't going very well. But I'm so not going to give up!

"Er, okay. But I, uh . . . well, you know, just started my . . . you know, and . . ."

Kevin's face turns bright red, and it appears his arm is suddenly very itchy. Bingo.

"Oh!" Maddie quickly opens her locker and shuffles her books around. "I get it. No problem. Let's go." She jumps up and kisses Kevin McGregor on the cheek. He looks even happier than when he scores a touchdown. Oh no. Derek's got mega competition.

My sister and I hurry out to her VW Beetle, which is conveniently parked in the front row of the student lot. Before she unlocks the doors, she says, "Wait a minute."

Now what?

"You're not going to make a mess on my seat, are you?"

Ugh. She's got a good point. I squint like I'm concentrating really hard. "Oh! You know what? I think it's stopped. Must've been a false alarm. Actually, I had my period last week." I laugh. "I don't know what I was thinking."

She shrugs and clicks her remote entry. We pile in.

"What's the deal with that Kevin guy?" I ask, digging out my iPod.

"I think he's going to ask me to homecoming!" She swipes lip gloss on her lips, throws the VW into reverse, and then hits the gas.

I do my best *I'm so not impressed* impression, complete with a partial yawn. "If you're crowned homecoming queen—which is all the buzz, by the way—you'll want to have the coolest date possible."

"People are saying I'm going to be the homecoming queen?" she asks, her voice juiced on hope.

I nod and slip on my sunglasses. They're all scratched up, but I love them anyway. I feel all 007 in them.

Maddie pulls out of the student parking lot. "Like who? Who's saying that?"

"Er . . . Yasmin. She knows everything about everything. She *is* the yearbook editor this year, you know."

Her freshly glossed lips curl up into her famously dazzling smile.

"You're not going to say yes to Kevin, are you?" I ask a few minutes later, as Maddie merges onto John Stockton Boulevard.

"What's wrong with Kevin? He's totally nice. He even checked my oil for me the other day 'cause I don't have a clue how to do that dipsticky thing. And God, he's hot. I seriously think he's the hottest guy at Snowcrest. Did you see his butt in those cargo shorts? Yum-mee!"

I shrug. "He's all right, if you like the tall, muscle-ripped, athletic type."

She smirks. "As opposed to the short, scrawny, couch-potato type?"

"It's just . . . you can't show up with the dude everyone is *expecting* you to go with. That would be as boring as Barbie going with Ken. You've gotta wow the entire student body with a mysterious, überhot guy—the guy every girl wants but only *you* can have."

Her green eyes grow a size. I must be finally getting to her. "Who should Barbie go with if not Ken?"

I blow my bangs out of my eyes. "I don't know—G.I. Joe? Darth Vader? But that's not the point. The point is, this is your last high-school homecoming *ever*. You want it to be perfect. Exciting. Romantic. Am I right, or am I right?"

When she pulls up the driveway, her cell

phone starts ringing. Maddie dives over my lap to grab her Nokia out of her backpack. "Kevin, hi!"

Oh no.

"Tomorrow night? . . . Yeah, that sounds way fun. . . . Okay . . . Buh-bye." She flips her phone shut and shuffles her Skechers excitedly.

"How was your algebra lesson?" I ask, desperate to get her mind off Kevin.

"Oh. It was great. Derek's really nice."

"And cute, too," I prompt.

"He's way smart."

"Don't you think he smells heavenly?"

"Yeah. He does smell good. I wonder what kind of cologne he wears. I've never smelled it before."

"I think it's Polo Explorer, if I remember correctly," I say, trying not to sound too obvious. "He said something about buying it the other day."

My sister shakes her head. "No, that's not it. That's the kind Kevin wears, and I'd totally recognize it. But who cares? Oh! I just thought of something. Derek told me he's all into fixing up cars. You should call him. I'm sure he'll figure out what's wrong with your scooter."

"Good idea. Will do."

"So, what's going on Friday night?" I ask as she pulls up the driveway and sets the emergency brake.

"A party."

"Oh? Where?" I unbuckle my seat belt.

"Why? Did you want to go? I could maybe get you on the list."

"There's a list?"

"Well, it's at Ruffalo's. You know, he lives in a gated community and everything."

"Wow. Okay. I mean, if you think it would be all right. I'd love to go."

"I'll just have Kevin leave your name at the gate. But you'll want to get your scooter fixed or ride with Yas or something, 'cause I'm going with Kevin. It's a date." She grabs her backpack and hops out.

I hop out too. "Okay, cool." Not cool, but at least I'll be there to run some more interference. And I've got to get some offense going, before Derek outright misses his chance.

Derek! What will it take to get him to go to the party?

I go straight to my room. Through the wall I hear Maddie chitchatting away on the phone, no doubt talking to one of her friends about the party, deciding what to wear and important stuff like that. Certain that it's safe for me to call Derek without her hearing, I pull my cell out of my backpack.

"Derek? It's me, Sasha."

"Oh, hi, Sasha." His southern drawl is even more palpable over the phone. If he weren't transfixed with my sis, I'd probably be swooning.

"Do you have plans tomorrow night?"

After a brief pause he says, "It depends. Are you asking me out?"

My breath catches in my throat. "Er, noooo. I was just wondering if you wanted to go to a party. Everyone's going to be there."

"Hmmm. I'm totally confused here. You insist you're not asking me on a date, yet this conversation bears a striking resemblance to one I had with a girl back in Texas, and lo and behold, it ended up being a *date*. A lousy one, but that's a different story."

"By *everyone*, I mean Maddie."

"Oh! Why didn't you say so?" I can all but see him grinning through the phone.

"But first I need you to do me a favor."

I ask Derek to pick me up and drive me to school so I can get my Vespa. Ten minutes later his truck pulls up the driveway,

Texas plates and all. On my way out I poke my head into Maddie's room. Per usual, various articles of clothing are strewn from one end to the other. She's sprawled out on her pastel-pink LoveSac, the cordless phone suctioned to her ear. When she sees me, she says, "Hang on," into the phone, and smiles up at me.

"Derek's going to take a look at my scooter now. See you in a bit."

She nods, pops her gum, and picks up where she left off: "The one with the green stripes, or the sheer one with little flowers?"

As Derek reaches over to open my door for me, Maddie watches from her bedroom window, her right hand gesturing like crazy as she gabs away. Derek's gaze fixes on her and a smile spreads across his face. I hope she can see him. He looks really cute in his faded Levi's jacket.

"She's on a quest to save the world, one bit of fashion advice at a time," I explain. I'm amazed how clean it is in here. Seriously, either he just got his truck detailed or he's a total neat freak.

Derek blinks as if he's waking up from a dream. "So, what's the deal with your wheels, Sasha?" He shifts the Chevy into reverse and eases his way down to the street. This old truck is surprisingly quiet, and no bumpier than Dad's Explorer. "Oh, nothing. I just got a ride home, so now I need a lift to pick it up."

"And your sister wasn't available?" he asks, steering toward the high school.

"You told her you like to fix cars, so I told her you offered to take a look at my scooter. Not that it's broken down or anything, but it's all in the game plan."

He turns to me and raises an eyebrow.

"Trust me."

"And is me going to this party Friday night 'in the game plan'?"

I nod. "Yup. Do you need me to come look in your closet, or can I trust that you've got something cool to wear?"

"Do you do that for all of your clients?"

"Whatever it takes." Not only do I get to choose an outfit I think his or her crush will especially like, but it gives me a chance to check out a client's bedroom. Based on all sorts of studies in this area, seeing someone's bedroom lends great insight into his or her personality.

I flip on his radio and static blasts into the cab. He reaches up to the volume knob, brushing my hand, and turns it way down.

"I haven't gotten around to figuring out which radio stations are any good."

"What kind of music do you like?"

"Just about anything. But not country, I beg you. I'm a recovering hick-music addict, and if I hear a steel guitar, I might jump on the bandwagon again. It's best not to risk it."

I try not to laugh, but I can't help it. "I think I might have seen you on *Dr. Phil* the other day."

When he smiles at me, his dimple appears on his left cheek. I hope my face isn't as red hot as it feels. I distract myself by filling his presets with the best radio stations.

"So I assume that purple thing over there all by itself is yours?" Derek asks, his truck chugging into the student parking lot.

"Yeah. The other cars are intimidated by it." He pulls up alongside my scooter, and I assign his last preset to my very favorite station.

"Who's that?" he asks, turning the volume up a notch.

"Nickelback."

Derek bobs his head to the beat, his hair falling into his eyes. "I like it."

"Yeah, me too." Oh, man. He looks so

adorable. *Focus, Miss Match.* Back to prepping him for asking my sis to homecoming. "Number one is the radio station you should have on whenever Maddie's in your truck." I press the first button and Prince serenades us. "Oldies but goodies."

He car-dances to "Kiss" while I reach for the door handle and jump out.

"Thanks for the ride, Derek. I'll pick you up at seven tomorrow night, okay?" I put on my helmet and wave.

"On *that*?"

"Are you making fun of my transportation?" I squint my right eye and purse my lips, challenging him.

He holds up his hands. "No ma'am!"

Of course I'm kidding; I know Yas will be up for driving, especially when I tell her we can play the Maddie's Little Sister card and get into a senior party. On the other hand, I have a feeling that being pressed up against Derek's body on this scooter wouldn't have been the most unbearable thing I've ever experienced.

Six

Hunter wrote me that Operation Paper Stick didn't go exactly as planned, but it did get Anna to notice him for the first time. In fact she got her first tardy 'cause she was chatting him up in the hallway. Now that's a success story if I ever heard one! He's totally psyched to see her again and eventually ask her out. I advised him to strike while the iron's hot, so we'll see what happens next. Finishing the e-mail, I type:

> Next time you see her, compliment her on a physical feature you find particularly endearing. Don't overdo it; it will make more of an impression on her if you concentrate on just one. Keep me posted!

Just as I send the message off through cyberspace, a *honk-honk-hoooonk* sounds from the driveway. Yas is here! I do a quick nose and tooth check in my mirror before bouncing down the stairs, zipping out the front door, and jumping into her Pathfinder. In the second the interior light is on, I see my best friend looking adorable in an emerald-green sweater and skinny black jeans.

"Hiya, darlin'," she says as I buckle my seat belt. "Oh my heck! You're all dressed up!"

I glance down at my red (slightly) off-the-shoulder sweater, knee-length skirt, and tall black boots. It took me hours to put this outfit together. Just once I'd like to have Maddie's or Yasmin's figure. They don't have to worry about finding clothes that camouflage their tummies and thighs.

"And is that *perfume* I'm smelling? What's the occasion, girl?"

I laugh. "No occasion. Just another super-hyped-up party at a rich senior boy's house."

"Whatever." She tunes the radio to 97.1 ZHT and starts grooving in her seat. Yas loves parties. Really, she loves any excuse to dance. And if no one's in the mood, she's famous for getting even the most hard-core couch potatoes and wallflowers shakin' their stuff.

"We're going to pick Derek up now." I tell her to turn up 5600 South and we drive east, the mountains growing closer by the minute.

She arches a meticulously shaped eyebrow (she swears if she misses a single day of plucking, she'll look like Bert on *Sesame Street*). "Derek?"

"Derek Urban. You know, the guy I'm fixing Maddie up with?"

"Ooooh, that's right. You've got so many clients, I lose track. Well, if you need any help with that tonight, I'm your girl."

"Thanks, Yas. You're a gem."

"By the way, this Derek guy is quite a hottie." She whistles.

I'm not about to confess to Yas that I also find Derek extremely good-looking. She'd make it out to be something much bigger than it really is and tell me I should drop the gig 'cause of a conflict of interest or some such nonsense. Knowing her, she might even refuse to help me get Derek and Maddie together, and I really need her assistance.

"Really? Huh. I guess I haven't noticed."

Yas harrumphs. "Any girl with halfway functioning eyeballs can see he's gorgeous."

Ten minutes later we're at Derek's. There's a long, winding driveway leading up to a grayish-blue ranch-style house. I can see a barn behind the fence, and though it's pretty dark, it looks like there are three or four horses prancing around back there.

A spunky Labrador barks his welcome as Yasmin's SUV comes to an abrupt halt. Derek opens the front door and yells something inside before running out. He's wearing a pair of faded Levi's and a vintage Firestone tee, his denim jacket in hand. "Mmm-mmm," Yas says under her breath. "You are most *definitely* blind, girl."

"Hands off, Yas. He's my sister's." I wink at her and then roll down the window. It's definitely getting cooler in the evenings. Good-bye summer, hello autumn.

He jogs up to the car and says, "Hey, Sasha. Does this look okay?" He gestures up and down his body, indicating his clothes. "Or do you want to come in and help me pick something out? You know, like you said?"

Oh, man. He looks perfect in what he's wearing, but I don't want to pass up the opportunity to check out his room. Despite the look Yas shoots me, I jump out. "This will only take a second," I tell her, and follow Derek to his front door.

A big candle is burning in the foyer, infusing the air with the scent of sandalwood and flitting shadows around. A stately grandfather clock tick-tocks from its corner of the living room, and I hear the droning of a TV somewhere in the distance.

"We haven't really had a chance to decorate," Derek says when he notices me looking around. He hooks his jacket on a brass coat rack.

I shrug. "It looks beautiful to me," I say truthfully. Sure, there aren't a lot of knick-knacks or pictures on the walls, but everything is very tasteful and functional.

"Derek?" a lady's voice calls from the back of the house. "Did you forget something?"

"Um, yeah," he answers. He leads me to the kitchen, which in contrast to what I've seen so far is very cluttered. Copper pans dangle from the ceiling, multicolored mugs and plates are stacked on the counter, and a mountain of veggies is sitting in the sink, seemingly waiting for a bath. A petite, curvaceous woman is watering one of a forest of houseplants. "Mom, this is my friend Sasha."

She whips around, clearly surprised her son isn't alone. "Oh, gracious! Well, Sasha," she says, wiping her hands on her pants, "it's wonderful to meet you." Her curly, reddish hair is adorned with a scarf, and a red leather belt accentuates her narrow waist. But it's her big, dark blue eyes—just like Derek's—that seize my attention.

"You too," I say.

"Well, we'd better get going," Derek says, starting down the hall. I follow, waving to his mom for good measure.

We walk past a few rooms and then into a small, tidy bedroom with a double bed and a cool window sitting area where he's laid his guitar. I flop onto the denim duvet while Derek opens his closet door. I quickly assess his room, hoping to glean any info that can help me in my quest to get Maddie to accept his homecoming invitation.

He doesn't have extra pillows on his bed, and from my research that means he doesn't need a lot of people around. He's perfectly comfortable having alone time, or being with just one or two others. And (awww!)

there's a teddy bear on his shelf that looks old and very much loved, which means he's sentimental and grounded. Oh, and that homework stacked neatly on his desk? That indicates that he's punctual. Which I already knew. To be honest I have no idea what the Bratz doll poking out from under his bed means.

"So, you want to take a look?" he asks, nodding at the closet.

"Sure." I stand and flip through a few of his shirts. "This one," I say, picking out a heather-gray golf shirt so soft I want to rub my face in it.

He nods and starts taking off his T-shirt. Oh my! He's changing right in front of me! Wait. I've already seen him shirtless in Synch Swimming. So why do I feel my cheeks flushing? Should I look away until he's finished dressing?

"What's this?" I ask, picking up the Bratz doll and admiring her chic karate uniform.

"It's my sister's. She likes to play hide-and-seek with it, and under my bed is her favorite hiding spot." He gives me this shy smile and reaches for the golf shirt that I'm clutching to my chest.

I hand it to him and return the doll to her hiding place. Then I turn on my heel, concentrating on the teddy bear on the opposite side of the room. "That's a cute bear. Did you have it when you were a baby?"

"Yeah. Poor guy's been through a lot. Snowball fights, baths, birthday cake feedings . . . you name it."

"Well, he looks pretty good, considering."

"And how do I look?" he asks, that shy smile unwavering.

I face him and nod approvingly. "Pretty good, considering."

"Considering?" he repeats.

"Considering your collar's all messed up."

He reaches up to fix it, but one side is still uneven. My Miss Match sensibility called to action, I walk over to him and smooth it out. "There, that's better." That instant a totally different sensibility takes over. I feel like one of those wives who help their office-bound husbands tie their neckties. Whoa! Where'd *that* come from?

"You smell good." He says it so softly, I'm not sure if he actually says it, or if my mind is just playing tricks on me. Then he takes my wrist, which I'm surprised to find frozen in its previous collar-fixing position, and holds it up to his nose.

"Thanks." I take my wrist back and smile at Derek, but I'm feeling extremely awkward. Or embarrassed. Or something like that.

As we walk out of his room and down the hall, I try to push these strange feelings aside.

"Derek?" his mom says as we pass by the kitchen. "Why don't you take some potato chips with you? I'm sure the kids will like that."

"That's okay, Mom," Derek calls, grabbing his jacket.

She materializes behind us, the bag of chips dangling from her outstretched hand. "Take them. And don't forget to tell Mr. and Mrs. Ruffalo thanks for having you."

Derek chuckles and takes the Lay's. "Yes, ma'am."

Once we're in Yasmin's Pathfinder, I introduce them. From the backseat Derek says, "And I thought Texas was famous for good-looking women. If my friends back home could see me now . . ."

I giggle and Yas flips her black hair the way she does when she's flirting with guys at dance clubs. "All *that* and a bag of chips," she whispers so only I can hear. I wink at her.

When we arrive at Ruffalo's neighborhood, the guard asks if we're on the list. I give him my name. He scans a piece of paper and then opens the gate, saying, "Have a nice night." I must say I'm impressed (and a bit surprised) that Maddie remembered.

Oh. My. God. I swear, this must be where all the Utah Jazz players live. I've never known *anyone* who lived in this area. Growing up, I always wanted to figure out how to get in for trick-or-treating 'cause it was rumored that they handed out ten-dollar bills instead of Smarties and Dum Dums.

A steady line of kids is filing inside a huge log-style mansion. Yas parks by the curb, and we all disembark from her Pathfinder. Old-fashioned street lamps—like the ones in those miniature-village scenes people arrange around their Christmas trees—illuminate the perfectly manicured lawns as we make our way to the party.

Ruffalo's front door is as big as most people's garage doors, and there's a slate waterfall in the entryway. A Kaskade CD is booming through the Bose speakers, and quite a few people are dancing on a Navajo rug in the living room. Yasmin finds her place in a group of gyrating girls, and Derek and I meander around the house in pursuit of Maddie.

"Are you sure she's here?" Derek asks as we search the den again.

And then I spot her. Well, various parts of her body, anyhow. Kevin's all over her like an octopus with separation anxiety. I don't think Derek's noticed her yet. Thank goodness!

"Hey, Derek? How about dropping off those chips and getting us some drinks? Looks like the kitchen's that way." I point to my left, sidestepping around him to block his view of my sis.

After he leaves, I walk up to the jumble of legs and arms and heads on the couch and tap on Maddie's shoulder. She looks up, startled. "Oh, hey, kiddo."

"Maddie? I know you're . . . er, *busy* . . . but do you think I could talk to you for just a second? I *really* need to talk to you." I paint a sad expression on my face and widen my eyes pleadingly. "Please? It's superimportant."

Maddie peels Kevin off of her and straightens her hair and skirt. She pats him on the hand and smiles. "I'll be back."

Kevin looks like he just watched BYU's football team clobber the U of U or something. Poor guy. "Sorry, Kevin. I won't keep her long," I say.

I drag my sister to the backyard—wow, a swimming pool!—and lead her to an empty table. The music is really loud through the outdoor speakers, so we have to practically shout. "What's wrong, Sasha?"

I scoot my chair closer to hers and then boohoo about the first thing that comes to mind: not having a date to the homecoming dance. "And it's my junior year, so I only have one more shot to go. What if I don't get asked next year? It would be a total tragedy!"

"I didn't know going to homecoming was such a big deal for you," Maddie says-slash-shouts.

"But it is! Everyone's going." I flail my arms around for effect. "I'm going to be the only girl sitting home that night, and it totally sucks."

I suddenly notice Derek behind Maddie, holding two cups. How long has he been standing there? I gesture for him to come closer. "Oh, hi, Derek!"

Maddie flips around. He holds one of

the drinks out to her and she grabs it with both hands. "Thanks. I was totally getting thirsty."

"No problem." Derek hands the other cup to me and takes a seat opposite us. He pins me with his dark blue gaze. "Is everything okay, Sasha?"

"Isn't the moon amazing tonight?" I ask breathily. "It's so *romantic*."

Derek and Maddie look at me kind of funny. "So, I guess you're not upset anymore?" Maddie asks.

Jumping to my feet I say, "I need to go to the bathroom. Be right back, okay?" I start walking away and flash Derek what I hope is a very encouraging smile. But then Maddie starts to get up. Oh no.

I jog back to the table. "Maddie, I'm not finished talking to you. Can you just wait a sec? I won't be long, I promise." I waggle my pinky finger at her (the "pinky swear" gesture we used to do as kids) until she slowly sinks back into her chair.

"Hey, Sasha!" Derek shouts. "Can you tell somebody to turn up the music while you're in there? I can barely hear it!"

Laughing, I head inside. Of course, I don't *really* go to the bathroom. I just want to give those two future lovebirds the chance to make a connection under this incredible moon.

Man, there are even more people in here now. I weave through all the bodies, nearly colliding with a guy carrying a case of beer. Where's Kevin? Hopefully, he's forgotten all about Maddie. And, more precisely, asking her to the homecoming dance. I find him hanging out in the kitchen, munching on the potato chips Derek brought. Kevin catches my eye, and before I know it, he's sidled up to me. Whoa, this guy's tall. "Where'd your sister take off to?" he asks.

"Uh . . ." While I'm thinking of something to say, Yasmin struts in to the beat of the music and grabs a can of Coke off the counter. "Hey, Yas! Come here!"

"Where's Maddie?" he asks.

"Kevin, have you met Yasmin yet?"

She sticks her bejeweled hand into the Lay's bag Kevin's holding and draws out a freakishly large chip. "I don't think so, but I've been dying to meet you. You played really great against Heritage last weekend."

While he stares at her, dumbstruck, she gives me a thick-lashed wink. Her hair is tousled (the only time I see it the least bit messy is when she's dancing), and her cheeks are sporting a radiant flush. The quintessential boy magnet. "I was just getting a quick drink, and then I'm going to hit the dance floor. Want to come?" she asks Kevin, nibbling on the chip.

He looks at me, then at her, and back at me. "Tell Maddie where I am, if you see her. I have something important to ask her tonight."

Oh, crap!

Seven

Derek and Maddie are still sitting at the poolside table, chatting. Maddie's leaning forward, which is a sign she's interested in whatever he's saying. Or it could be a sign that she can't hear him over this deafening music.

I can't keep fighting Kevin off. He's determined to ask Maddie to the dance, and she's going to say yes, and that will be it for Derek. More than that, it'll be Miss Match's first flat-out failure to deliver.

No! I can't let that happen. This has *got* to work out. I approach the table, listening in case I can pick up on any of their conversation. But of course the music's too freaking loud.

Maddie looks up. "Hey, sis. So, you ready to finish our talk?"

"Uh, actually, I'm feeling a lot better now." I stand taller, square my shoulders, and beam at her. "There's a bowl of peanut butter M&M's in the kitchen." Okay, so I didn't really see any. But there *could* be, and they're Maddie's favorite. She takes the bait.

"Well, Derek, it's been great hanging out with you. I'll see you inside," Maddie says.

"How'd it go?" I ask Derek as soon as Maddie's gone.

"She's really nice. Like you."

I smile. "Good. I was hoping you wouldn't change your mind about her, you know, once you got to know her a little better." I scoot my chair beside his and lean in close to him. Man, if my next boyfriend smells half as scrumptious as Derek, I'll be in heaven. "I need to tell you something. There's a guy named Kevin who's hot for Maddie, and I know he's going to ask her to the homecoming dance tonight. You've got to beat him. You've got to ask Maddie first."

"Tonight?" Derek taps his fingers on the table and shifts in his chair, apparently distracted.

Putting my hand on top of his, I give him a no-nonsense look. "Yes, tonight. The sooner the better." I stand and pluck a bunch of flowers from the huge clay pot by the pool. "Take these."

He rises and stares at the flowers in my hand, frozen. What, is he nervous? Is he having second thoughts?

"Derek, I'm sure she's going to say yes." I take a step closer and have to tilt my head up to meet his eyes. In the moonlight, his eyes are a deep midnight blue. "But if she says yes to Kevin, she's not going to say yes to you." I hold out the makeshift bouquet.

"This isn't how I wanted to ask her, Sasha. I wanted to ask her in a special way. I've been planning . . ." He takes the flowers and stares at them, his temples pulsating. A moment later he turns away from me and takes a few steps toward the swimming pool. Some guys are splashing around, trying to get Kennedy to jump in.

"I'm sure it's a great plan, Derek. You're sweet like that. But—"

"It won't be the end of the world if she goes with Kevin," he says over his shoulder. "I'm just not ready to ask her." He lays the flowers in the pot and walks into the house. He doesn't look back, not even when Kennedy does a cannonball and screams hysterically 'cause the water's so cold.

After we take Derek home, Yas says, "Sheesh. He got all quiet all of a sudden. He just sat back there and gnawed on a toothpick the whole ride home. Did Maddie give him the cold shoulder?"

I sigh. "No. I think she might be into him. Trouble is, Kevin's into *her*. And Derek doesn't seem like the fighting type." We drive a few miles, coming into the bright lights of Salt Lake City.

Yas pops a piece of Orbit in her mouth and passes me one. "Well, he's definitely not into me."

"Derek?"

"No. Kevin. I got him dancing, but it was like he thought I had cooties or something."

Huh, that's bizarre. Typically, guys are way touchy-feely around her, and she has to keep swatting them away. "I bet that was refreshing," I say, trying to put myself in her adorable polka-dotted flats.

Yas's mouth drops open, revealing a wad of mint-green gum. "*Refreshing?* Try humiliating!" She screeches to a halt at the stoplight and flips down her vanity mirror. "Am I losing my touch? Am I suddenly butt ugly? Am I hideous?" She snaps the visor back in place and then shudders. "Do I have BO?"

I pretend to sniff her armpit and she pushes me away, laughing. "Babe, you're as hot as ever," I say. "There's definitely something wrong with that boy."

Hang on a sec. Could it be? Is Kevin so into my sister he can't even dance with another girl? Or is he just afraid that Maddie's the jealous type, and he didn't want to risk her seeing him dancing with another girl 'cause she's his first choice of homecoming date?

Right before Maddie and her friends leave for the movies Saturday night, I snap a picture of them. She looks so cute in her new trousers, and I think Derek might appreciate seeing the photo. So I e-mail it to him, hoping it will inspire him to pop the question sooner rather than later. However, I never hear a peep from him the whole weekend, and he's not in chemistry Monday morning.

I hope he knows I'm not giving him a refund just because he's dropped off the face of the earth.

Yeah, right. Who am I fooling? I'm worried about the guy. This isn't like him.

Ten minutes before the school day is officially over, I'm sitting in English class. We're supposed to be writing about our favorite Edgar Allan Poe poem or story, but I'm just doodling. It's completely quiet in here, except for the occasional paper shuffle or chair scoot. I'm finding it hard to concentrate on my journal entry, 'cause I'm still wondering why Derek isn't at school today. Did I freak him out or push him too hard? I was just trying to keep it real. If he wants to go to homecoming with Maddie, he's got to act fast. I don't want him to miss out on his chance, that's all.

I happen to glance out the little window in the door just as Kevin and two of his jock pals walk by with a big black trash bag. Oh no! What are they up to?

I spring up, grab my backpack, and scurry to the front of the classroom. The teacher looks up from a gargantuan book and peers at me over his reading glasses. "Mr. Schockley?" Though I'm whispering,

I know the entire class is listening in. "I totally spaced that my mom's picking me up early from school for a doctor's appointment. Is it okay if I go a few minutes early today?"

He jiggles his jaw, which incidentally jiggles his chins. (That's right, plural.) I smile and tilt my head a little to the right, hoping to appear every inch the angelic student.

"All right, Miss Finnegan. But next time, let's get a note from the attendance office."

"Yes, sir." I swing open the door and run in the direction the boys were heading, right to Maddie's locker. One is fooling with her combo while the others are taking all sorts of balls out of the bag.

"What are you guys doing?" I ask.

Looking startled, Kevin straightens and tucks a basketball under his arm. "Just decorating her locker. Don't worry about it." He shoots me a *stay out of it* glare and proceeds to stuff her locker with the balls.

"I never heard of the football players decorating the cheerleaders' lockers," I say. "Isn't it, you know, the other way around?"

Kevin strokes the beginnings of a goatee with his free hand. "That sounds a little sexist, don't you think? Here at Snowcrest, we are an equal-opportunity sports program." The guys snicker and I roll my eyes.

"Perhaps you should take lessons on decorating lockers from the girls, then. A bunch of random balls doesn't exactly say, 'Good luck cheering,' or whatever."

Kevin opens his mouth to say something—

"Two minutes!" one of the guys warns, tapping his watch. They cram the remaining balls in as quickly as possible. Then Kevin slams the locker, sticks a sign on the door, and they all disappear around the corner.

The sign reads: *I didn't have the balls to ask you in person. Will you go to homecoming with me? Kevin.*

I'm so not kidding.

I peel the sign off and pull out my cell. Yasmin's number goes right into voice-mail. Crap. I punch in Derek's digits. *Please, Derek, answer.* No luck. The hall is suddenly jammed with people, and the sounds of voices, lockers banging, and someone's rap music fill the air. I glance over to where Kevin is waiting and see his head pop around the corner for a split second before going back into hiding.

Come on, Miss Match, think of something. Anything!

Maddie is heading straight for me, a textbook clenched to her chest. She's laughing at something her friend Jenny has just said. She suddenly stops laughing and points at something by the doors on the opposite side of the hall. Something I can't see from where I'm standing guard over Maddie's locker. Everyone freezes, staring at whatever she and several others are pointing at.

Clop, clop, clop.

What the——?

I'm about to abandon my post to see what's captured everyone's attention, when a real live white horse trots into the hall, someone dressed like a knight on its back. The horse is so tall, and looks so out of place at Snowcrest High School. Its long white mane and tail are brushed, and a red blanket with a gold shield emblem is draped over its back. The rider is wearing full knight apparel: from mask to body armor to metal boots. But instead of a sword or shield, he's holding a bouquet of yellow daisies.

Daisies? Could it be . . . ? Oh. My. God!

The knight looks up and down the hall

and then steers the horse right for Maddie. By now a crowd of teachers has gathered. Maddie looks around her nervously, clutching her book to her chest even tighter. When the knight holds the flowers down to her, her face turns cherry red. I run up to her as she takes the bouquet. There's a note on it: *Dear Princess, I'd be honored if you'd accompany me to the homecoming dance.*

She starts giggling and Jenny starts shrieking. The shrieking is contagious: I think I'm even doing it.

But Mr. Green, the principal, isn't sharing in the excitement. "Farm animals are not allowed on school grounds. Remove your helmet at once."

Derek does as he's told, his dark blue gaze set on the still-blushing Maddie. "Well?" he asks her.

Maddie does a bit of a guppy impersonation before saying, "Yes!"

The crowd goes wild, whistling, clapping, and cheering. When they finally settle down, Mr. Green asks, "What is your name, young man?"

He grins. "Derek Urban."

"Derek Urban, you are suspended for a whole week. Get that animal out of the building immediately." Next he turns to Ms. Whitehead, his secretary, and says, "Contact his parents."

Everyone boos, even some of the teachers. But Derek's still smiling as he puts his helmet back on. He gives his horse a kick and heads out, the clopping of hooves echoing magnificently in the otherwise silent school.

Her eyes all starry, Maddie practically floats to her locker. In all the excitement I totally spaced Kevin's ballsy invitation. Maddie opens her locker, releasing the bouncy avalanche, sidesteps a soccer ball, and goes on with her business as if her locker being stuffed with balls is an everyday thing. She puts her hand to her heart and sighs, "The most romantic invitation to a dance in history . . . and it happened to *me*." Then my sis twirls on her toes and drifts over to a group of squealing cheerleaders, who are no doubt waiting to get the scoop on her mysterious knight in shining armor.

I watch the girls leave, feeling a sense of pride and accomplishment. Yet another satisfied client for Miss Match. Now I can go home and choose another case to work on.

However, when I see Kevin, his head down, one hand stuffed in his pocket and the other grasping the garbage bag, I wipe the grin off my face.

This victory for Derek equals a major loss for Kevin. And I can be sure this five-star athlete isn't used to losing.

"Want some help?" I ask. "With the balls?"

He shrugs his left shoulder. "Suit yourself."

Most of the balls have gathered by the Western Civ classroom, across the way. We throw the balls in the bag, one by one. I keep replaying the whole knight scene in my mind. I can't believe Derek came up with something so original and romantic all by himself. No *wonder* he didn't want to ask Maddie to the dance at Ruffalo's party last Friday. And he totally broke school rules to ask her. The poor guy's suspended for a whole week!

How cool is that?

"Hey, are you going to put that football in the sack, or are you keeping it as a souvenir?" Kevin asks.

"Oh, here. Sorry." I toss it over.

When we've picked up the last ball in

sight, the bag is only half full. "Someone must've kicked your balls down the hall," I say.

He snorts. "You can say *that* again."

I'm sitting on my Vespa, putting on my helmet, when my cell phone rings. "Hey, Sasha! I saw you called. Sorry I missed you," Yas says.

"No biggie, girl. Guess what?"

"Can we skip the part where I have to guess and you just tell me straight up?"

"Oh, okay." I take a deep breath. "Derek asked Maddie to homecoming . . . and she said yes!"

"Wait a minute. Is this the knight in shining armor thing? I heard about it from Brian. I guess some guy came riding—"

"Yes! Isn't it awesome?"

"You get better at your matchmaking gig every day."

"Actually, the knight thing was his idea. I had nothing to do with it," I admit.

"Wow."

"I'll say. So now that that case is all wrapped up, want to celebrate?"

"But it's Monday."

"Let's go to Starbucks and see if there

are any cute U of U guys there," I suggest. "My treat."

"Okay. I just need to freshen up real quick and then I'll be there."

"Freshen up" is Yasmin-speak for "brush hair and teeth, gargle some Scope, reapply eyeliner and lipstick, spritz on some perfume, and change into a totally new outfit (including switching handbags when germane)." I think getting ready is a pain in the butt one time a day, let alone two or three. But that's just me.

So anyway, I've got at least thirty minutes before Yas will be there, plenty of time to buzz over to Mrs. Woosely's house real quick.

"Who is it?" Mrs. Woosely hollers after I bang the brass knocker on her front door.

"Sasha Finnegan," I answer, straightening a flamingo that's all lopsided. Only now it makes the others look skewampus. After tilting a couple more pink birds this way and that, I realize my efforts are futile and surrender. "Don't worry. I'm not selling magazine subscriptions or wrapping paper for my school."

The door swings ajar, and she promptly invites me in. Mrs. Woosely is wearing a quilted velour warm-up set, her hair in painful-looking pink curlers. "Do you like 'em?" she asks, lifting her right foot with what appears to be tremendous effort. "I think they're funny-looking, but I hear they're very popular these days. That's what my son told me when he gave them to me."

I take in her bright yellow Crocs and nod. "They're all the rage." Like ten years ago, but hey. They *are* comfy. "Well, here's the last of what I owe you." I hand her the money Derek paid me, feeling the sweet sensation of closure.

She flips through the bills and gives me a funny look. "This is too much."

"Well, consider it interest. I really appreciate your letting me do this on the downlow, Mrs. Woosely." I turn around and start down the steps.

"Well," she says, peering over my shoulder at my scooter, "how about you keep this, put it toward a car? You're gonna catch a humdinger of a cold on that thing." She smacks the money in my hand and practically pushes me out the door.

"But I . . ." It's obvious by the way her eyes are narrowed and her bright yellow foot is tapping that this woman won't take no for an answer. So I just thank her and wave.

Once I get to Starbucks, there's an impressive line of patrons waiting to order their übercomplicated coffee concoctions. I decide to wait it out and take a seat at a table at the front of the shop. From here Yas and I can scope guys both inside and out.

The man at the next table looks up and smiles at me. He's grasping his cup of coffee, a northern Utah real-estate guide spread out in front of him. He's got the whole professorly look going on: the wool blazer, the slightly wrinkled chinos, and metal-framed glasses. His longish brown hair is mussed and a bit gray around the temples. Even though he's ancient, he's cute in a way. Not my type but . . . oh my gosh! Totally Mom's type. And as an added bonus he's not wearing a wedding band.

I scoot my chair closer, slipping into Miss Match mode. "Excuse me."

He turns the page in his guide before looking up.

"I, uh, noticed you're looking at houses in the area?"

"Yes, I am." He takes a tentative sip of his coffee.

"Are you new in town?"

"I've been working at the university for a couple of months."

"Ahhh. Well, if you don't mind my prying, do you have a real-estate agent? I mean, if you're working at the U, you're probably way too busy to navigate the housing market by yourself. I know an agent who is practically famous around here. And not only will you like the houses she'll show you, I guarantee you'll love the company."

His lips curve into the cutest smile. "That's a pretty big promise, young lady."

I shrug. "She's the best. Well, I'll let you get back to your reading." Then I scoot my chair back to my table and wait. One, two, three . . .

"Do you have this real estate agent's card, by chance?" Now that he's standing up, I can see he's about six-foot-one or -two. A few inches taller than Dad. Mom would look so adorable standing beside him.

"I thought you'd never ask." I reach in my purse and hand him Mom's card. He studies the picture and flips the card around in his fingers a couple of times before slipping it into his wallet.

On his way out he tosses the real-estate guide into the recycle bin and gives me a little wave.

"Who was that?" Yas asks, pulling up a chair. "Don't tell me you were flirting with him. I mean, he's handsome in a Harrison Ford way, but he's old enough to be your father."

"Or my mother's new boyfriend."

Yasmin laughs, tossing her freshly brushed hair. "You never stop."

Eight

The doorbell rings. "I'll get it! It's for me!" Maddie screams, racing to the front door. Okay, so I get she's a cheerleader, but she's acting a bit overzealous, even for her. I turn down *Oprah* and listen.

"Hey, Maddie."

Derek?

I spring off the couch and follow them down the hall and into her room. Her room is totally clean. Her algebra textbook is on the bed, which is perfectly made. Does she have a maid I'm not aware of?

"So you've moved the algebra lessons to the house?" I ask.

"What's up, Sasha?" Derek nods at me politely. He's wearing a forest-green shirt that makes his eyes appear darker than usual.

"Derek's suspended from school, so we figured it includes the library." Maddie sits down and pats the bedspread beside her for Derek to join her. I take that as my cue to leave them alone.

"Well, let me know if you need anything . . ." I find myself saying.

"How about a couple of Cokes?" Maddie says, opening her book.

I go to the fridge and raid the soda dispenser. Before I make the delivery, I check my appearance in the living room mirror. Oh, joy. There's a zit on my chin as red as the Coke cans. No wonder no one has asked me to homecoming.

"Here ya go, kiddies." I place the sodas on Maddie's desk.

They're so into the FOIL method they don't even look up.

Now what?

It's not like I can watch *Oprah* when Derek's here. He'll think I'm a total dork. Maybe I'll go to my room and start on a new Miss Match gig. Might as well put a little more money in the bank, right? It really would be nice to have my own car sometime this millennium.

While I'm booting up my laptop, I hear

Maddie cracking up. I've heard that girl laugh a million times a day, every day of my life. Why does it bother me so much right now? What is Derek saying—or doing—to make her laugh so much?

Why do I care?

I shake my head, hoping to oust those thoughts from my mind so I can concentrate on my latest matchmaking gig. Beth Samuels is a shy photographer-slash-poet, a sophomore who's into Goth. I think she's probably pretty behind all that makeup, and she's got one of those awesome raspy voices like Demi Moore. She's crushing on this junior called Jasper, who as she tells it is a brooding artist type. A painter. They both go to Murray High, just south of Salt Lake. I decide to take advantage of the whole art angle and type the following e-mail:

Subj: Important Message from M.M.

Date: Sept. 23, 4:56 PM Mountain Standard Time

From: MissMatch@MissMatch4Hire.com

To: Goth1900@kmail.com

Dear Beth,

It was great to meet you, and I look forward to working with you.

Due to the nature of my service, I cannot guarantee the exact result you are seeking, but I guarantee I'll do everything in my power to make your dream of going to the Mayhem Festival with Jasper come true. That said, I have some ideas to put things in motion. Please send me a poem of yours that you'd like him to read, as well as a photo of him doing something he loves.

Ciao for now,
M.M.

"Sasha! Maddie!" Mom yells, and about gives me a coronary. What's she doing home so early? "Where are you two?"

"I'm studying!" Maddie shouts back. Ha. I'm sure Mom's having a coronary over *that* one.

I hit send, then scurry out to the living room.

"What's going on, Mom?"

She runs her hand through her hair and gazes out the window into the street. "Well, I never imagined I'd be saying this to my teenage daughter, but . . ."

"Out with it, Mom. I can handle it."

Slowly, she turns around to face me. She inhales and then exhales so hard her bangs puff up. "I'm going on a date tonight."

Oh my gosh! "Really?"

"Really."

"Really?" I can't believe it!

She smiles. "*Really*."

"So . . . who is he?"

"A very nice man named Holden Clark. I was showing him some houses today, and—"

"Does he work at the U?"

She tilts her head. "Well, yeeeees . . . but how did you know that?"

"Er, well, I just recognized his name from . . . an article about a professor of . . ."

"He teaches economics."

"That's right. Economics. So? You were saying?"

"We got along really well, and we were so busy looking at houses that we skipped lunch, and we were both getting hungry, so he asked if I'd like to have an early dinner with him tonight, and . . ."

"And?"

"And I said *yes*, that we could discuss some properties on the outskirts of Salt Lake that might be more affordable. But he just shook his head and said that he'd talked about houses enough for one day and wanted to talk about . . ."

"What?"

"Me." He wants to discuss *her* over dinner. How sweet!

I jump up and down. "That's great!"

"Is it?" She tucks a strand of brown hair behind her ear, suddenly looking worried.

"Of course it is. Now let's go and pick out something for you to wear," I say, steering her down the hall to the master bedroom. "You're gonna be a regulation hot mama."

"Why did you lie to me, Sasha?" Yas shoots me a look from hell over her strawberry TCBY smoothie.

"What are you talking about?"

"You said I'm as hot as ever. You know, after Ruffalo's party. When I tried to help you out by keeping Kevin away from your sis and he wouldn't touch me with a ten-foot pole . . . ?"

"You *are* as hot as ever, Yas." How can someone so skinny and beautiful have such a complex? Isn't it Shakira who goes to a therapist to deal with the trials of being gorgeous? Puh-*lease*. Try being curvy or (heaven forbid) fat. Or butt ugly or deformed, even. Now, those are *real* issues. Not being skinny and beautiful.

"Then why the heck hasn't anyone asked me to the homecoming dance?" she asks.

I shrug a shoulder. "I don't know." Since there's a Jazz game tonight, the mall is a virtual graveyard. After I helped Mom get ready for her date, I asked Yas to meet me at TCBY. She hates basketball and loves dessert, so I knew I could count on her. Admittedly, I was desperate for some company, but had I known she'd dive right into homecoming *this* and homecoming *that*, I would've been better off at home with my World Geography textbook. "No one's asked me, either."

"But you don't care. You're strong like that, Sasha. You don't equate your self-worth to how many times you get asked for your phone number or invited to school dances."

Interesting. My best friend believes I'm eager to join a convent or the local chapter of Spinsters of the World. But I don't have the energy to argue. Besides, isn't this precisely the image I'm going for? That guys are great for most girls, but for me they're just a big waste of time? "Sounds like you've been watching too much *Dr. Phil*, chica." I take a huge bite of frozen yogurt and immediately wish I hadn't. Mega brain freeze. *Owwwwww.* Blinking back the tears, I try to keep my face from contorting into some-thing out of a Tim Burton movie.

"Tell me why no one's asked me." She points her extra-long plastic spoon at me accusingly.

"Someone *is* going to ask you, Yas. You just have to be patient." I'm putting my money on Brian, but if that falls through somehow, find-ing someone else will be a piece of cake.

She sits up straight. "Really? You know this? Is he just being shy or something?"

Oh, man. Talk about an insta–mood upper! I can't tell her it's just a bunch of inspirational hoopla. What's the harm in going along with her fantasy of a mysterious future homecoming date? She's my best friend, after all, and I can't bear to see her all depressed like this. "I can't say. Sworn to secrecy."

"Just answer one question. You know, on account of us being best friends." She sticks her spoon into her cup, and her ruby red lips curve into a coy smile. "Is he hot?"

"You'll see," I say with a cheesy wink.

She stands up and takes my arm. "Don't just sit there! We've got to find me the per-fect outfit for being asked to homecoming."

Yas flips through the Nordstrom racks with an urgency that's borderline scary.

After an hour of trying on clothes, she's tossed several outfits onto the *it works* pile.

"Do you need help narrowing it down now?" I ask, hanging up the heap of *it sucks* stuff.

"I'll just get all four," she says, zipping her jeans. "After all, I have no idea which day he's going to ask me, and I don't want to be caught in some outfit I've had for months."

"Yeah, that's true." God, I hope I can get someone to ask her. I make a mental note to start working on Brian first thing tomorrow.

> Subj: Hi from Sasha
> Date: Sept. 24, 6:45 PM Mountain Standard Time
> From: MissMatch@MissMatch4Hire.com
> To: 66Chevy@kmail.com
>
> Hey Derek,
>
> I was just getting ready to close out your account and I wanted to make sure you're perfectly satisfied with your Miss Match experience.

Ugh. That's totally lame. I delete it and start over.

> What's up? I haven't talked to you in a while, what with you getting suspended and everything. And

when you came over yesterday, I was really too busy to chat. Anyway, I've been taking notes for you in chemistry so you won't be too behind when you come back Monday.

Of course, if you need a private chemistry tutor, I'm all yours. It's the least I can do since you're helping Maddie so much. She got a B+ on her last algebra quiz. I don't think I've ever seen Mom so happy. Or Maddie. So thanks.

I know you're going to have a great time at the homecoming dance with her. My last bit of advice is to wear a tie that doesn't clash with pastel pink. She hasn't bought her dress yet, but I guarantee it'll be pink.

Well, I guess that's it for now. Have a good night.

xoxo
M.M.

Oops. I delete "M.M." and type:

Sasha

Before I lose my nerve, I hit send. A couple minutes later there's a message in my inbox. Wow, that was fast. Oh. It's not from Derek.

Subj: Re: Question from M.M.
Date: Sept. 24, 6:56 PM Mountain Standard Time
From: Goth1900@kmail.com
To: MissMatch@MissMatch4Hire.com

Dear Miss Match,

I wrote a poem about him last summer. Here it is:

"Rain"
The world is washed gray
Soggy
Moody
Smiles are fragile and quick to vanish
Kids stay inside
Hiding
Sodden cats seek shelter under eaves
Surviving
When will it end?
Dirt, oil, fallen leaves slosh down the drain
Eyes open
The world is washed clean
Ready to start anew
Ready to be with you

~Beth

Hmm. Okay. We can make that work. I visit a few of my favorite blogs for about ten minutes, in case Derek writes me back. But he doesn't, so I fold my laptop and walk into the kitchen. As I'm sprinkling coconut on the fruit salad, Maddie comes bounding in, wearing her red SHS warm-ups. "What's for dinner?"

"Shish kebabs on the George Foreman."

"Mmm. Sounds fancy."

I stir the salad, careful not to smoosh the bananas.

Maddie hops up on the cabinet and swings her legs. "Can you believe Mom's dating?"

"It's bizarre, all right. But I'm happy for her."

"Me too."

The garage door groans, and a few seconds later Mom is in the kitchen, kissing us on our cheeks. She has a healthy radiance about her, like she's been on a cruise or something. And if my nose can be trusted, she drenched herself in Obsession perfume.

"So, did you see him again today?" Maddie asks.

"Who?" Mom's blush gives her away. She totally knows who Maddie's talking about. "Oh, Holden?"

"Yeeeees," I say. "Unless you're dating multiple men these days."

Laughing, Mom opens the fridge and unearths a Dasani. "Well, I don't know if Holden and I are *dating*, per se, but he did call and ask me out to dinner again."

"When?" Maddie jumps down and starts setting the table.

"Tonight. But I thought I should, you know, play a little game of hard-to-get."

I nod my approval. "Good thinking, Mom."

"Actually, it was Maddie's suggestion."

Maddie holds a fork up in the air and gestures with it as she speaks. "I might not know much about school stuff, but I'm a genius when it comes to dating. We'll have this guy eating out of the palm of Mom's hand in no time flat."

Will Maddie have Derek eating out of the palm of her hand?

Is he already?

I log on to the Web and check my inbox one more time before hitting the sack. Nothing besides the spam we all know and hate. I delete it all and check once more for any new messages before powering down my laptop.

As I wiggle down into my comforter, I can't get Derek out of my mind. People at school are still talking about his amazingly romantic knight story. It's weird, but I totally miss seeing him in chemistry. Sure, I saw him a little yesterday when he came over to tutor Maddie. But it's not the same when she's around.

I sigh and twist over onto my side.

When he's with Maddie, he's so into her. Which is good, right? I mean, he *did* hire me to get her as his date to homecoming. And they're going. It's what Derek wanted. His wish came true. And obviously Maddie wants to go with him, or she wouldn't have accepted his invitation. I close my eyes and relive the whole knight-in-shining-armor scene in my mind. Only this time I'm the princess holding the bouquet of daisies, and Derek's asking *me* to go to the dance.

Whoa, Sasha! Focus. This is about Maddie and Derek.

What's going to happen the day after homecoming? Are they going to date? Be boyfriend-girlfriend? Is Maddie going to say, "Thanks for the dance; now I'm outta here"? Oh God, if she does that, she'll totally break Derek's heart.

But that's beyond my control, right? I did my job, which was to get them together.

I realize it could've happened without Miss Match's help. Who knew Derek was such a romantic? Who knew he was such a . . . great guy? Well, anyway, I can't control what happens to them beyond homecoming, so there's no use worrying about it.

Why is it that when I'm with Derek, and Maddie's not, I feel like I'm the only girl in the world?

Sheesh. That sounds so freaking lame. What, am I in love with the guy? Puh-*lease*. I hardly know him. And he's with my *sister*, for heck's sake. My beautiful, skinny, popular, happy sister.

I squish my pillow just right and lay down again. Headlights dance across my walls and then disappear entirely. Why won't these weird feelings just disappear?

Right then and there I make a pact with myself. I will turn my attention to matters besides Derek. My job is done, and I wash my hands of him. Oh, sure, I'll still be his friend. I mean, we *are* lab partners and fellow synchronized swimmers and all. So! Friends for the sake of getting good grades, and friends since he'll be taking my sis to homecoming. But that's all. I'm sure the universe will provide plenty of stuff to keep my mind occupied. Bring it on!

"Mom, what the heck's wrong with you?" It's about three o'clock Monday morning, and she's wrapped up in a blanket on the couch, staring into space with puffy, bloodshot eyes. Her cheeks are tear-stained, and her lips are a thin, quivering line. *Bewitched* is on late-night TV, and it's turned up way too loud. "Are you sick?"

Maddie wanders in, clutching her pillow with one hand and rubbing her eyes with the other. "Is it Holden?"

Thunder booms outside, and the pounding of rain sounds like there are fifty people hammering on our roof. I shiver.

Mom blinks several times and then grunts as she sits up. "No, Holden's great. I'm great. I'm going to bed now."

Maddie and I watch as Mom zombie-walks to her bedroom. I click the remote, and the TV screen goes black and silent. Her door creaks shut.

I pick up the blanket and start folding it. "What do you think is going on?"

Maddie shrugs. "Maybe a big sale fell through."

"Maybe, but I don't think so. I haven't seen her this upset since Dad sent her the divorce papers."

"Well, I guess we'll just have to tie her up by her toenails in the morning and demand she tell us what's wrong," she says.

"Maddie?"

"Hmmm?"

"Do you like Derek?"

She crinkles her nose and then allows a little grin to escape. "Sure. He's really sweet. And he's a great tutor."

"Are you, you know, *excited* to go to homecoming with him?"

"Yeah, I guess so. I mean, if it gets boring or anything, I can always hang out with the gang. They'll all be there. *Everyone's* going to be there." She looks at me, her sleepy green eyes studying my face. "Why are you asking me these questions?"

I shrug and focus on the rug. "No reason."

"Sasha, you told me at Ruffalo's that you were feeling better about not going to homecoming. Is that the truth, or did you just say that so I wouldn't worry?"

Before I meet her eyes, I make sure I'm smiling in a way that makes me look confident. "It's the truth." Then I use Yas's words: "I don't equate my self-worth with how many times I get invited to school dances."

She angles her head and scrutinizes me. I must look convincing, because she says, "Okay, then; 'night," yawns loudly, and retreats to her room.

I sink onto the sofa and gaze out the window. It's so dark outside, not even a sliver of the moon showing. Water patters on the panes.

Why do I feel like crying?

Nine

"Hey, Sasha. Long time no see." Derek slides his chair beside me. I'm so beat I could just crash right here in chem class. I was up all night worrying about Mom and wondering—despite my attempts not to—whether Maddie is going to break Derek's heart like she's done to so many guys before him.

Derek, on the other hand, looks happy and rested, like he just got back from spring break or something. Something like a week's suspension.

Mr. Foley weaves up and down the rows of tables, handing back last week's Charles's Law labs. A red A-minus is scribbled on mine.

Derek peeks at my paper. "Nice work."

I shrug. "I guess." I made a stupid mistake converting Kelvin to Celsius—off by one. Shoot.

Derek lowers his voice. "Is something wrong, Sasha?"

"No, why?" Should I ask him if he got my e-mail? Not that it was a big deal or anything. But it would've been nice to get a response of some sort.

"I don't know. You're just acting all weird."

My cell phone rings. The room grows ominously quiet, and heads swivel in my direction. Wonderful. I dig the shiny red culprit out of my backpack and glance at the caller ID. I do a double take. Dad? What's *he* calling me for?

Mr. Foley stalks over and holds out his hand. "Hand it over, Miss Finnegan." Under different circumstances I might be pleased he actually knows my name. I'd do anything to be invisible right now.

I press the power button. "I'm so sorry, Mr. Foley. I just spaced turning it off. It won't happen again."

He leans so close to me I can see his nostril hairs. "The phone."

I sigh and surrender it.

"You can come for this after school." He holds my phone high in the air, the scapegoat for all naughty cellular devices of the world.

"You can use my cell to call back who- ever it was," Derek offers once Mr. Foley is a safe distance away.

"Thanks."

After class I take Derek up on his offer. His cell phone is ancient, but it works.

"Smith and Jenson Advertising," a woman's nasally voice says. "How may I direct your call?"

"Richard Finnegan, please."

"One moment."

I wait two or three minutes and mouth "sorry" to Derek, who's waiting patiently by his locker. Finally, she comes back on the line. "I'm sorry, but he's not answering. Would you like his voicemail?"

I sigh. "Can you check Valerie's office? He's been known to spend time in there."

"Uh, okay. One moment."

"Valerie Kensington speaking," my dad's girlfriend answers all importantly.

"It's Sasha. Is Dad there?"

"Oh! Actually, he is. Here you go."

"Hey, kiddo," my dad says. "I was

just calling to see if you're free for dinner tonight. Seven o'clock at P.F. Chang's."

"You called me at school and got my phone confiscated just to see if I wanted to go to dinner?"

"Oh, I'm sorry, honey. So are you available? Maddie is. I got ahold of her already."

"Oh, all right." At least I won't have to cook tonight.

"See you then."

I hang up and pass Derek's phone back to him. "Thanks."

"No problem. And thanks for your chemistry notes." He blinks his dark blue eyes. "Are you sure you're okay?" Despite the wall I've tried to put up around my heart, his soft southern drawl makes my stomach flutter.

"Totally," I say, smacking a smile on my face. "You know, just parental stuff."

"Okay. Well, let me know if I can do anything." He puts his hand on my shoulder, instantly sweetening my sour mood.

Speaking of mood makeovers, what's up with Dad? He sounded so . . . *giddy*. Maybe he got a promotion and a big fat raise. You know, since he's sleeping with the boss and everything.

Maddie, Dad, Valerie, and I are sitting at a table by the window at P.F. Chang's. A steady line of parents and children amble down the street, bundled up against the chill. Not that it's weird to see a ton of kids anywhere in Utah, but I bet something like *Disney On Ice* is in town. I used to love those shows when I was a kid.

Dad ordered a glass of chardonnay for himself, Sprite for Val, and an assortment of appetizers. Maddie is slurping her Diet Coke through a straw, and I'm nursing a steaming cup of jasmine tea. There hasn't been much conversation. Judging by the way Dad and Valerie keep exchanging loaded glances, however, I have a feeling things are about to get interesting.

"We have an announcement to make," my dad says, beaming. Valerie's tentacle-like fingers cover his hand like a sea anemone preparing to feast.

"We know you two are living together," Maddie says cheekily. "We're not stupid."

I kick her under the table.

"Ow!" She narrows her eyes at me.

Dad clears his throat and refreshes his smile. "Actually, it's more than that. You see, Valerie and I are very much in love and . . ."

Oh, God. Why haven't I noticed the diamond ring on her finger before now?

I think I'm going to puke. I wonder what lettuce wraps will taste like coming back up?

Valerie takes a big gulp of soda and closes her eyes while she swallows. Next, she scoots out her chair and stands. Smoothing her blah Ann Taylor suit, she takes a deep breath. Her whole production seems to have captured the attention of even the Chinese warrior statues guarding the front door. "As your father was saying, we're in love. And last night he proposed to me."

"You said yes?" Maddie asks.

"Yes, we're getting married," Dad says. "December fifth."

"Don't you think that's a little rushed?" I say. Not to mention the ink on our parents' divorce papers isn't even dry yet.

"Well, girls, the wedding isn't our only news," Dad says softly.

"We're having a baby!" Valerie announces with a happy, full-body wiggle.

Maddie knocks over her glass, and a sticky, brownish-black tidal wave drenches the Peking dumplings. I do a jaw status check and realize mine's flapped wide open. But I can't quite seem to reel it in.

"You two will be big sisters." Gee, thanks Dad. As if we didn't already figure out that part.

I'm too stunned to speak, but Maddie's not. "But you're too *old* to have a baby." This directed to both Dad and Valerie. Guess she didn't see the article about that sixty-seven-year-old Romanian woman.

Valerie eases into her chair and gives us her *let me explain this so a kindergartner can understand* look. "We weren't exactly trying to have a baby, but now that it's happened, we consider this a gift from God. A blessing." Who does she think she is, the Virgin Mary?

Dad adds, "We're very excited to bring a baby into the world. And we couldn't be more pleased that you two are sharing in our joy."

"What? We're not joyful; we're *shocked*," I hear myself say. "Haven't you ever heard of birth control?" Man! I ask the universe to send me something to take my mind off Derek, and it provides, all right.

The server, who had the extreme misfortune to stop at our table during my little outburst, turns on his heels and hurries back to the kitchen. Smart man.

Valerie turns to my father. "Don't worry, dear. They're right. This is quite a shock for them. Let's give them some time to let it sink in." Then she turns to Maddie and me, and an enormous smile erupts beneath her reconstructed nose. "Richard, signal the waiter. I'm positively starving. You know, eating for two is hard work. So, are you girls ready to order?"

Um, yeah. Like I really have an appetite now that I'm sitting across from my dad and the plastic-surgery-enhanced boss he had an affair with and consequentially knocked up. Oh, man. Just wait till Mom hears!

"Mom!"
"Mom!"

Maddie and I race into the house, finding her in the living room in front of the TV. She sits up, looking alarmed. "What is it?"

Maddie flops on the couch next to her. "Dad and Valerie are having a baby!"

Mom presses the mute button on the remote. Then she slouches into the cushions and heaves a huge sigh. "I know. He told me on Sunday. I . . ."

I shed my parka and take a seat. As I take Mom's hand, I wonder how it would feel to have your husband cheat on you with his boss and then drop the baby bomb. Is this why she was so upset last night? "Weird, huh?"

"Yeah, weird," Mom says, her voice a bit hoarse. "So, are they getting married? I didn't ask, because I didn't think I wanted to know. But I guess now that the initial shock has worn off, I'm curious."

Maddie and I look at each other. "Yes," I say. "And soon. You know, so she won't be as big as a house when she walks down the aisle."

Maddie says, "They'd better get married tomorrow, then. Did you see how much food she ate tonight? More than the entire Snowcrest football team, I'd guess."

"Do you know when the baby's due?" Mom asks.

Maddie and I shake our heads. "We were too busy freaking out to get the particulars."

"You two are going to have a little sister or brother," Mom says with quite a bit more enthusiasm than I'd expect.

"Oh, great." Maddie rolls her big green eyes.

"We're both old enough to be its mother."

"Neither of you is allowed to even think about having babies until you're thirty-five." Mom cracks a smile. "I'm *much* too young to be a grandma."

We all laugh. "So, whatcha watchin'?" I ask, turning the volume back on.

"*Sabrina*. It just started."

Maddie and I snuggle into Mom's sides and watch with her. When the credits finally roll, I say good night and go to my room. I'm about to power down my laptop when I see there's a message in my inbox.

Subj: Re: Hi from Sasha
Date: Sept. 28, 9:51 PM Mountain Standard Time
From: 66Chevy@kmail.com
To: MissMatch@MissMatch4Hire.com

Dear Sasha,

I'll definitely try and scrounge up a tie that won't look terrible with Maddie's dress. You're really great at your job, you know that? Anyway, just wanted to say thanks. For everything. You're the best.

Your humble chemistry lab partner,
Derek

I should've known Derek's homecoming invitation and consequent suspension would be the hot topic in our Synch Swimming class. Once we all jump into the pool, the freshman girls circle Derek and Maddie like a shiver of hungry sharks. I watch from a safe distance, treading water. Maddie is loving the attention, smiling and nodding in agreement with what they're saying. Conversely, Derek is all fidgety, like he's big-time uncomfortable. All of a sudden he dives underwater and resurfaces in the middle of the pool. We share a brief smile before he swims his perfect butterfly to the far end.

After we all swim twelve laps, Coach White blows her whistle. "Okay, folks, listen up. Time to break into your groups and work on the skills we learned last week. Remember, the three-minute routine you perform for your final is eighty percent of your grade, so from here on out no horsing around."

"Sir Derek, Great Knight of Snowcrest. No *horsing* around!" Trinity giggles hysterically at her little joke.

Derek shakes his head good-naturedly, bless his heart.

I'm hanging onto the side of the pool,

refusing to laugh along with the other girls. I just did ten laps of freestyle and two 'fly, instead of my usual breaststroke-sidestroke combo. It was kind of nice being one of the first ones to finish, though I think Derek might've finished one or two laps ahead of me. Then again, he did have a head start.

After the class gets its collective giggles out, it breaks into threesomes and foursomes. When Maddie jumps out to fetch our nose clips, I notice that Derek is standing by the windows, looking around like he's lost.

"Yo, token male," I say, all smart-alecky. Derek whips around, giving me a lopsided smirk. "Yeah you, in those hideous green goggles. Get over here. You're on our team."

"Oh, yeah? How'd you two get so lucky?" Derek adjusts the waistband of his shorts, revealing that sexy muscle that slopes diagonally from hipbone down to . . . his nether regions. Mmmm, not bad. I'm just about to tear my eyes away (I'd be mortified if he noticed me drooling), when he jumps into the pool, splashing water all around me. When I open my eyes, he's standing right in front of me. I mean *right* in front of me. A droplet of water drips off a strand of his hair, falls on my shoulder, and slides down my arm. My heart is palpitating so fast and I'm so breathless; it's like I just swam another dozen laps. I think he might be staring at my lips, and this totally bizarre, bubbly sensation floods my entire body, and I can't help but wonder: What would it be like to kiss him?

When Maddie says, "So, Sasha, we'd better get Derek up to speed . . ." it sounds like she's miles away, in a tunnel or something. But her voice, and the fact we're now a triad, jostles me back to reality.

I lick my lips and try to wipe the blush from my cheeks. "Yeah, okay."

I go through the motions, laughing at Derek's zany attempt at a "ballet leg," all the while wrestling with what just happened between the two of us. My sensible side has its say: Derek jumped into the pool and surfaced closer to me than expected. The look on his face, and how he kept standing so close, without moving back—that was 'cause he was surprised, that's all. Right? I mean, it's not like he has any interest in me. He's into Maddie. In fact, I tell myself in the utmost of strictness, *Maddie* will find out what it's like to kiss Derek, not me!

I'm trying to move on with my life, but that pesky romantic side won't let this go. It insists something happened between Derek and me just then. Something, I don't know, *special*. And it doesn't help that Derek keeps looking at me. I mean, really *looking*, like he's searching for something in my eyes.

Coach White blows her whistle, and we all climb out of the pool. I wrap my towel tightly around my body. It's the Care Bears one Derek borrowed, and as soon as I'm tucked away in the ladies' locker room, I can't help holding it to my nose. It smells like that scrumptious cologne he wears. Girls are giggling and chattering all around me, scrambling to get a shower, but I barely notice them.

I'm dinking around on my computer Friday night, looking through old account records to see if anything that worked for other clients might work for Beth, when I get an IM notification.

```
PrincessYasmin[7:38 PM]: U studying?
MissMatch[7:38 PM]: No
PrincessYasmin[7:39 PM]: Working?
MissMatch[7:40 PM]: Not really
```

I can't say why, but I'm having a hard time getting into Miss Match mode these days. I must be getting lazy or something. I mean, I haven't even closed out Derek's account yet, and Maddie accepted his invitation to homecoming twelve days ago. Not that I'm counting.

```
PrincessYasmin[7:42 PM]: Brownnosers
playing at the Depot tomorrow night.
PrincessYasmin[7:43 PM]: I just won 2
tix from 97.1
MissMatch[7:44 PM]: So we're going?
PrincessYasmin[7:46 PM]: It's our
destiny! Only I'll have to meet U
there, so I'll leave UR ticket in
UR mailbox.
MissMatch[7:46 PM]: Cool
PrincessYasmin[7:48 PM]: Gotta go 2
stupid piano lessons, C ya later
MissMatch[7:49 PM]: Later
```

"Sasha, I'm leaving!" Mom hollers down the hall. "Don't wait up."

Having a mother in the dating scene is totally bizarre. But hey, I'm just glad it's going so well so far. I peek out my window and see an old black BMW in the driveway.

Holden looks dapper in a long gray trench coat, and Mom looks darling in her fuzzy faux-leopard jacket and black ankle boots. Is that a white long-stemmed rose she's sniffing? Oh, wow. Props to the prof!

I'm about to power down my laptop when I get an awesome idea. I should work it out that Brian Goldman goes to the Brownnosers concert. Yas will be totally in her element, and Brian will definitely notice what a hottie she is shakin' her stuff on the under-twenty-one dance floor. After Miss Match works her magic on him, he'll surely ask her to homecoming.

Even though she hasn't come out and admitted it, I really think Yasmin's into Brian. And she wants to go so bad, she'll definitely accept. It'll be a done deal in a matter of a couple of hours. Perfecto!

Hey! While I'm at it, I might as well get Beth and Jasper to go to the concert, too. That way I can hit four lovebirds with the same arrow, so to speak. Dang, I'm good.

I e-mail Beth right away and tell her the plan. Next, I look up Jasper's contact info on Beth's account. I pick up the phone, and after pressing the caller ID–masking code, I dial his phone number.

"Hello?" a guy answers.

"Is this Jasper?" I ask, trying to make my voice sound womanly.

"Uh, yeah. Who's this?"

"This is Micki Monroe from 97.1 ZHT. You're on the air, Jasper. I've got great news for you. You're our Friday night winner!"

"Huh? What did I win?"

"You won a ticket to the Brownnosers concert tomorrow night!"

"Who?"

"Brownnosers."

"Never heard of 'em."

"Well, after tomorrow night you won't be able to forget them. They're the hottest new band to cross the Utah border, my friend. Now hold the line and we'll get your info. And thanks for listening to 97.1!"

"I don't. But thanks anyways."

I wait a moment or two and then say, a bit more calmly: "Jasper, we're not on the air anymore. May I please get your last name?"

"O'Neill."

"I'll have a ticket waiting for you at the Depot's will-call—"

"Wait!" he interrupts. "Did you say one ticket, or two? I mean, it's not like anyone wants to go to a concert by himself."

Right. Yas did say she won two tickets, not just one. I clear my throat. "Good point. That's right, we radio stations usually give tickets away in pairs. Okay, Jasper. Two tickets it is! Have a grrrrreat time!"

I hang up the phone and grin. That was a piece of cake. So easy, in fact, I do an encore for Brian Goldman.

Brian is quite a bit more excited about being a "big winner" than Jasper. It makes me want to be a deejay so I can hand out free concert tickets to unsuspecting listeners. Oh, and nonlisteners, in Jasper's case.

Beth writes me back and says she's free but will have to find someone to drag with her so she doesn't look like a total loser. I guess this band doesn't exactly jibe with her Goth lifestyle. Ah, the things we do for love.

While I'm online, I hit the Depot's website to order the tickets.

Oh no.

How can this be? I mean, my plan was going along so well until now. How the heck am I going to get six tickets to a sold-out concert?

Ten

First thing Saturday morning I grab the ticket Yas left for me out of the milk box. Too bad I don't know any magic tricks to make this baby multiply into six. After breakfast, I drive to the Gateway and go directly to the Depot ticket booth. There's got to be *some*thing I can do to get my hands on some Brownnosers tickets.

The ticket guy looks up at me, and recognition flashes in his chocolate eyes. "Miss Match?"

"Shhh!" I shoot him a warning glare and look around, making sure no one heard.

Poor kid's got red face issues. "I'm . . . sorry. I wasn't thinking. I was just so surprised to see you here."

"It's okay, Caden. No harm done. So, how are things with you and . . ." *Come on, Miss Match. You've got to remember who you fixed him up with.* ". . . Ashleigh?"

He smiles. *Whew.* "She's great. We're going to homecoming next weekend and everything."

"Cool." Does everyone have to keep pounding it in that I'm the only person on the planet not going to homecoming? Well, Yasmin isn't going yet, but that's a big ol' *yet.* When I'm finished with Brian, she'll be golden.

"Oh, I wanted to thank you for referring my service to Derek."

Caden laughs. "Oh yeah. Derek. I met him at the athletic club. That boy has high aspirations, but hey. I thought if anyone can get the job done, it's you. So how can I help you?"

"Well, you see, I need six tickets to the Brownnosers tonight."

He shakes his head. "No can do. It's been sold out for weeks."

I exhale loudly. "It's really important, Caden. I'm working tonight, if you catch my drift. Just think how tragic it would've been had a little thing like tickets gotten in the way of me fixing you up with Ashleigh."

He purses his lips and wiggles his mouse to activate the computer screen. "I'd really love to help you out, especially since you've done so much for me . . . but there's not a single ticket left."

"Isn't there something I can do? Do employees get free tickets? Maybe I could apply for a job here."

"No, that won't work. We have a pile of apps a mile high." He reaches for a Kleenex. When he's finished blowing his nose, he says, "But I just thought of something . . ."

"Tell me!"

"JMR is one of the sponsors, and they're having a big contest down at Pine Woods Mall today. They're giving away tickets. I heard about it on the radio last night."

I go up on my tippy-toes. "Awesome!"

Caden cranes his neck to see the clock behind him. It's ten forty. "I think it starts at eleven, though."

"Wish me luck!" I say, then haul ass through the shopping center. I don't even have time to ask or worry about what the contest is. I've got to blaze if I'm going to make it across the entire city of Salt Lake in twenty minutes.

A huge, rowdy crowd swarms the JMR store, gathering around orange cones. Jace Evans, one of the ZHT deejays, is on a small stage. He's wearing his trademark snowboarder goggles and a putrid green Hawaiian shirt. He taps the mic several times and then announces, "We've got five and a half minutes till we're live, folks. Will the contestants please line up at the north side of the fountain?"

I shove through the throng. About twenty or thirty people in all sorts of swimsuits are lined up by the fountain. I tap the guy at the back of the line, a guy who happens to be sporting a super-sized Roxy bikini. With green and yellow butterflies. "What's going on?" I ask.

"We had to change into a swimsuit off JMR's clearance rack, which was pretty picked over." He shifts his top and grimaces. "Now we're just supposed to wait for instructions."

I ask, "What do you win?"

"Tickets to the Brownnosers concert tonight. Other stuff too."

"That's cool."

"I've just *gotta* win a ticket to the concert. The Brownnosers are my all-time fave band, but I didn't have enough money to get a ticket when they first went on sale, and by the time my paycheck came, it was already sold out. I've been a fan of the Brownnosers since, like, forever!"

I swear, the kid would still be blabbing on had Jace Evans not intervened. Jace's voice booms, "Two minutes, folks." Shoot. It's not enough time to change into a swimsuit.

When it appears no one's watching, I poke my nose down the front of my hoodie. Black bra. Doesn't look much different from that purple bikini top that gal with the dreadlocks is sporting. Then again, that girl has the cutest figure. I don't.

Oooooooh, man. What a numbskull not to check if there were tickets available! Dumb, dumb, dumb!

Well, I've already gotten myself into this mess. I can't give up now, not even in the case of my extreme body anxiety. If these people don't like the way I look, it's their problem.

After taking a deep and very shaky breath, I peel off my hoodie and yoga pants, tucking my purse underneath. I hide behind Roxy guy in my black bra and panties, biting the heck out of the inside of my cheek. *Please, God. Don't let anyone I know be here. I'll go from being Maddie's Little Sister or Yasmin's Friend to That Chick Who Wears Her Bra and Panties in Public.*

"This is Jace Evans, live at JMR in Pine Woods Mall. We've got a whole slew of contestants dressed in stylin' JMR bathing suits, psyched to find out what their challenge is going to be. Since we're giving away tickets to the sold-out Brownnosers concert, as well as some other killer prizes, it's not gonna be easy. Only the most physically fit, the most daring, and the most aggressive shall emerge victorious." He cues the music guy, and a few minutes of *Star Wars*–like music blasts through the mall.

Come on, Miss Match. Win for Yasmin. Win for Beth. Win for love.

A huge bouncer type hauls out a JMR shopping bag and pours thousands of coins into the fountain. My heart beats like crazy in anticipation.

I tune in to what Jace is saying: "When I give the word, the contestants will jump into the fountain and scoop up as many coins as they can. There are twenty-four pennies made in the year that the Brownnosers played their first concert. Each of these winning pennies is good for a free ticket to tonight's concert at the Depot. The remaining pennies are good for other prizes, including CDs, DVDs, MP3 players, and of course cool JMR clothes. And everyone's a winner. The suit you're wearing is now and forever yours."

Roxy guy yanks his bikini bottom out of his butt crack. "Great, just what I always wanted."

"So what year did they play their first concert?" I ask him.

"2006." He blows a strand of hair out of his eyes, looking very determined.

"Ready, set, go!" Jace shouts, and the swimsuit people jump into the fountain, splashing and screaming like toddlers in the kiddie pool.

I scoop up some coins and sift through them, hanging on to the one penny I found. It's a 2005. My heart sinks.

Before I have a chance to grab any more, I'm up to my elbows in bubbles.

Roxy guy, who's been diving into the water to search for pennies, surfaces, rubbing his eyes. "Dang!"

"To make this a tad more challenging,"

the deejay's voice blares over the commotion, "we've added detergent to the water. Thirty-two ounces of Tide, to be exact."

I jump out of the fountain, scramble through the crowd, and wave at Jace Evans to get his attention. "Hey, Jace! Can I use your goggles?"

He smiles down at me. "That's what I call game." He pops them off and tosses them to me. "Now, bring those back, or I'll hunt you down."

I turn and start running back to the contest, my competitive spirit trumping my phobia of wearing my undergarments in public. But then Jace yells, "Nice panties!" and I'm embarrassed all over again.

Come on, Miss Match! You can do it!

Back in the fountain I dive underwater and weave between people's swishing hands and hopping feet, the pennies shining at me like beacons. I check the dates of the pennies as I find them. 2000, 2005, two more 2004s. Where the heck are the 2006s?

I stand up and toss the pennies to the opposite side of the fountain, hollering, "Pennies up for grabs!" The contestants go bonkers, shoving and wading around. Leaving me room to search. For a millisecond, anyhow.

Then I find my first 2006. I want to break into a celebratory dance, but I promptly refocus. One down, five to go. Luck does come in threes, because in no time I've found two more.

An enormous girl sideswipes me, and I fall into the water with a big splash. "Are you okay?" someone asks, and I feel a tight grip on my upper arm. When he comes into focus, I see that it's Roxy guy. His bikini top is untied, and his entire body is white-washed with suds.

"Fine, fine!" I think my lip is bleeding, but I don't care. I've got to find more 2006 pennies.

A skinny redhead in a striped tankini jumps up and down, crying, "I found one! I'm going to the concert!" A couple other girls circle around her, wanting to see one of the much-sought-after coins.

I swipe my hand over my lip. My hand turns a pinkish color, blood mixed with soapy bubbles. Suddenly, this whole plan seems ridiculous. If there are only twenty-four tickets to win, the odds of me finding any more are slim to none. And speaking of slim, I'm feeling like an elephant among gazelles in my bra and panties.

But I'm not ready to give up. Not yet.

As long as there's still a chance, I'm going for it.

I plunge into the water and immediately score another winning penny. And another. Oh my God—I only need one more!

Roxy guy leaps up into the air like he's spring-loaded. "YES!" He pumps his fist into the air. Despite my competitive attitude I smile at him, feeling genuinely happy he found one.

Jace says into his microphone, "Looks like the competition is winding down, folks. If you're holding any pennies, please bring your coins to the table to my right and claim your prizes." Several people in ZHT tees spread beach towels around the fountain, some to step on and some to wrap around our wet, soapy bodies. The people behind the orange cones lean in to ask the contestants what they've won.

The fountain empties, except for a few diehards (including *moi*) who aren't ready to throw in the proverbial towel. If there's just one more 2006 penny in this water, I'm going to get it. I'm scooping pennies like crazy, not caring one iota about any prizes other than the tickets. There have *got* to be a few more left.

I swim around the fountain, Jace Evans's goggles protecting my eyes. But all I spy are silver coins. I guess I should be elated about winning five of the twenty-four tickets. Right? But I wish I could've found one more. . . .

"Everybody out!" the deejay orders, and Usher's "I Can't Let U Go" blasts from a forest of nearby speakers.

Just my luck there aren't any towels left, and I have no clue where my clothes or purse ended up. Making my way to the prize table, I stop in my soggy tracks. Standing right in front of me, waving, is none other than Derek Urban.

I snap off Jace's snowboarding goggles and peer down at my soapy, underwear-clad, shivering body. Oh, great. My skin is all splotchy-purple. Of all the people to see me like this, why Derek?

"Hiya, Derek."

"Looks like you gave everyone a run for their money."

"You watched?" Does my face look as mortified as I feel?

"Sure. It was very entertaining. You did a bang-up job on your torpedo sculls, Sasha. Coach White would've been so proud."

I laugh. "Well, maybe if you vouch for me, I can get extra credit or something."

"So, what exactly did you win?"

Thankfully, I don't have to answer, because a little girl materializes at his side just then. He ruffles her curly blond locks. "This cinnamon-and-sugar-coated little darlin' is Sami. My sister. She's shopping for a new pair of boots, but we got sidetracked when she spotted the Auntie Anne's pretzel stand."

She's simply adorable: big bright eyes, front teeth MIA. She smacks her lips and cocks her head at her brother. "Yeah, well, *he* needed new underwear."

Derek chuckles. "Can't be going around commando, you know." I blink a couple of times, trying to erase the not-so-horrible image that popped into my mind.

"Cute suit, by the way," Sami says, checking out my bra and panties. "Where'd you get it?"

"Er, Victoria's Secret?"

Thank goodness the line moves up, and it's my turn. A woman in a ZHT visor is holding her hand out, waiting for me to cash in. She takes my pennies and nods. "Not too shabby, young lady."

I take my five concert tickets and turn back to find Derek, but he's disappeared. Oh well. It's not like I wanted to hang out and talk to him in my dripping wet underwear. At least the Speedo I wear for Synch Swimming covers my tummy.

The bathing-suited contestants raid the JMR store, taking turns using the dressing rooms to change back into street clothes. I search around the front of the fountain, but Derek isn't the only thing that's disappeared. Where the heck are my clothes? Is this somebody's idea of a sick joke?

"How'd ya do?" Jace Evans's smooth deejay voice comes from right behind me.

"Oh, well, okay, I guess." I feel like the morning of my sixteenth birthday, when I was expecting a car but Dad bought me a Barney scooter instead. Well, maybe not *that* bad, but still. I'm majorly disappointed to come this far and not fully succeed.

He eyes the stack of tickets in my hand. "I'd say you did a little better than okay."

"Thanks for letting me use these." I smile and pass him his goggles.

"No problemo. It's nice to see the world in its true colors from time to time. You know, instead of neon orange."

"So, are you going to the concert?" I ask, jerking my head to get the water out of my ears.

"I was going to, but my girl's got a ballet recital, so I'll probably pass. Why? Were you hoping I'd be there so I could buy you a drink?"

Oh my God. I'm sure I'm blushing. "Er, noooo. I'm not legal yet. But I was wondering if you have a spare ticket?"

"Boy, are you greedy." His words surprise me, but he's smiling as if to add *no offense.*

"Well, believe it or not, it's not for me."

He strokes his goatee, his eyes mere specks behind his orange goggles. Slowly, he reaches into his wallet—one of those beat-up leather ones attached to a big silver chain—and extracts a ticket. He waves it in front of my face. "But first you have to do something for me."

I raise my eyebrow.

"Tell me what you're doing with all these tickets."

I shift my gaze left and right. "I . . . can't."

"Why not? I'm just curious, that's all."

"Really, I can't."

"Well, at the risk of sounding like your mother, you should probably be getting dressed," he says, jumping down from the stage. "It's a little cold out for damp underwear."

"Uh, well, actually . . ." I look around, hoping my clothes have miraculously reappeared in the last two minutes. No such luck. However, I do see Derek and Sami coming over, a Dillard's shopping bag in his hand. "I don't have any clothes. Someone must've taken them."

Trying to keep a straight face, Jace grabs an extra-large 97.1 ZHT tee out of a box and gives it to me. He holds my tickets while I slip it over my head, thankful to be hiding my body after so much unnerving exposure. I still can't believe Derek saw me like this. I don't think I've ever been so embarrassed.

"You didn't hide my clothes, did you?" I ask Derek when they join us at the fountain.

He chuckles. "Sadly, I never had that stroke of genius. But I can definitely help you look." While Sami perches on the fountain ledge and Jace busies himself with deejay cleanup duties, Derek and I buzz about, searching for the missing clothes and purse.

About five minutes later Derek runs over, my yoga pants and purse in his hands. "Are these yours?" he asks.

"Oh my gosh, Derek. Thanks so much!" I say, stuffing my legs into my pants as quickly as I can. "Where were they?"

"Over in that tree," he says, pointing with his chin.

"I don't suppose there was a yellow hoodie with a dragonfly on the back stuffed in the bushes?" It's one of my favorites, but I'm happy to finally be dressed, and I know I'm lucky no one took off with my purse.

He shakes his head. "Sorry." He peels off his A&M sweatshirt and hands it to me. "Here you go." I pull it over my head, over the radio station T-shirt and my damp bra, and I'm instantly ensconced in warmth.

"Thanks, Derek. For everything."

"No worries. So, do you want a ride home?"

I would love a ride home in Derek's old pickup, but I've got to deliver these tickets to the Depot, and I can't divulge all my Miss Match plans to him. "No thanks, I'm good. You've already done so much."

"Don't mention it." Sami yells something about getting going so she doesn't miss something Hannah Montana—ish on TV, and Derek says, "Well, see ya later, Sasha."

"Later." I watch Derek and his sister disappear into the hustle and bustle of the mall. I pull the hood over my wet head, inhaling the clean masculine scent that is Derek. But there's no time to revel in stupid fantasies. I've got to get these tickets to the will-call!

Oh, man. I'm one ticket short, so I guess I won't be going to the concert. Hopefully, the love connections can happen on their own, without my assistance. *Will Yasmin be pissed if I give my ticket to Beth?* I wonder, adding my ticket to the stack.

"Can I get some will-call envelopes?" I ask Caden back at the Depot ticket booth.

"You got the tickets?" he asks, eyes wide.

I fan out the tickets to show him before stuffing them into the envelopes. Two for Jasper, two for Beth, and two for Brian. Wait a minute. Where'd this extra one come from? Did Jace Evans slip his into the stack when I was putting on this T-shirt? I'm sure I'm smiling like a monkey, but I can't help it. My plan is working out after all! Jasper and Beth and Yas and Brian are going to be together in no time.

I take a deep breath, the October air crisp and tingly. Yep, love is definitely in the air. At least for some people.

Eleven

Why didn't anyone tell me you're supposed to wear black? Yas is all sexy in a black shift minidress and killer knee-high boots, and everyone around us is in head-to-toe black. Except the bouncers, who opted for dark green. But even *they're* wearing black pants. I'm wearing a yellow voile blouse and faded flare jeans, which seemed like a decent outfit at the time. But now I feel like Mandy Moore in a sea of Avril Lavignes. Oh, joy. I'm getting a mega headache, and it's not from the pounding bass.

"Hey, you in the yellow! Are you gonna order something or just stand there looking dazed and confused?" the scruffy guy at the under-twenty-one bar yells at me.

"I'll have a . . . Diet Coke?"

"Make that two," Yas shouts over my shoulder, giving the bartender a smile that's been known to turn guys to mush. I just hope it turns one Brian Goldman to mush.

We grab our drinks and head toward the stage. Yasmin works her way to the epicenter of the dance floor and does her stuff while I scope. Aha! I recognize Jasper from the yearbook photo Beth provided and feel a surge of Miss Match adrenaline.

Now to find Beth.

I weave through the crowd, getting closer to Jasper. The opening act, a band called Firesticks (if I'm to take the big red FIRE-STICKS painted on the drums as a hint), wraps up, and Brownnosers takes the stage. I've heard *of* Brownnosers, but I've never actually *heard* them. They wait till the hooting and shouting dies down a notch and then launch into their first number: a bouncy song with loud drums and hyperactive sax, the singer practically choking on the mic as he wails his jumbled lyrics. That's when the crowd goes *really* wild. I take this opportunity to "accidentally" bump into Jasper.

"You okay?" he shouts over the commotion.

"Hey, you look totally familiar. Do you go to Murray High?"

"Yeah. Do you?"

"So you know Beth Samuels?" I ask, simultaneously dodging his question and getting to the point.

He fiddles with the ring in his eyebrow. "Yeah, I think so. Isn't she that chick who always looks like she's going to a funeral?"

His friend pipes in, "Or a Halloween party?" They chuckle and kind of bump elbows.

Ugh. Not good. "She's actually really cool. Anyway, I'm just looking for her. I'm supposed to meet her here."

"Oh." Jasper shoves his hands into the pockets of his baggy jeans.

"Well, I'll go make the rounds again. If you see us, come over and hang out."

"Uh, okay." I shoot him what I hope is a superfriendly smile and take off across the floor. I've just spotted Brian by the door. Looks like he missed the black-attire memo too.

"Brian! How are you?"

"Oh, hey, Sasha."

"It's so good to see you. I didn't know you liked the Brownnosers."

"I don't really. I just won a pair of tickets

last night, so I thought I'd check it out. You know, since it's free and everything."

"Gotcha. Well, Yasmin's going to be totally psyched you're here."

He looks around and tugs at the cuff of his rusty-orange shirt. "She will? Why's that?"

"Because she was going to invite you. But I made her take me instead, on account of being her best friend and all." I give him a big toothy smile.

"She was going to invite me?"

I roll my eyes in a silent *duh* and wait for him to pay the bartender for his soda. "So, are you going to the homecoming dance with anyone?"

"I don't think so."

"Why not? There are so many hot chicks dying to be your date. You shouldn't be so selfish."

He laughs. "Oh yeah? Tons of hot chicks? Name one."

"Yasmin."

He stares at me, speechless.

"But she's getting sick of fending off other would-be dates, so you'd better ask her right away," I add.

"Hey, Sasha." I turn and end up face-to-chin with Derek. How random is this?

I mean, I keep bumping into him. Earlier today at the mall (in my wet bra and panties, no less) and now here at the Depot. It's almost like he's . . . Nooo. It's just a weird coincidence.

Boy, does he look hot in that black pec-hugging sweater and those ripped Levi's!

Struggling to wipe the surprise off my face I ask, "What are you doing here?"

He squints his dark blue eyes at me like I've just asked the dumbest question. "Going to a concert?"

I laugh. "Right. Well, me too . . ."

"Aren't you a little overdressed?"

Glancing down at my outfit, I shrug. I mean, it's not black, but it's not exactly my Sunday finest, either.

"This morning you were parading around in your underwear." Derek glances over at Brian, who's suddenly interested in our conversation. Sensing that we're about to become Snowcrest High School's next hot topic, Derek chuckles and adds, "Or so I hear."

"So you guys know each other?" Brian says. "Oh, that's right. Derek's taking your sister to homecoming." He slugs Derek on the shoulder and Derek grins.

"And we have chemistry together," he says.

"Chemistry *class*," I'm quick to clarify.

So Brian's friends with Derek? Not sure how that slipped by me. Hmm. Well, I'd be happy to hang out with Derek for the rest of my life, but I've got to get back to work. "If you'll excuse me, boys, I see someone I need to say hi to. Then I'm going up to dance with Yas." I point to the stage and make sure there's a flash of *hot dancing chick who apparently likes me* recognition in Brian's eyes. "You should join us."

Then I hightail it over to Beth, who's hiding in a corner with another raven-haired girl. It's no surprise that Beth got the black-attire memo. She probably typed it up and distributed it.

Wow, it's *loud* over here. Guess that huge speaker is the perpetrator. Beth says, "Hey," and mouths "Is he here?" when her friend bends over to tie her shiny Doc Martens.

I nod.

Her friend whips up and looks me up and down. And down and up. "Who's the flower girl?"

Beth puts a hand on her stud-belted hip. "She's the daughter of one of Mother's friends."

Her friend snorts. "Figures."

I take a deep breath. *Don't get all offended. Just do your job, Miss Match.*

The Brownnosers wrap up their song, giving our ears a courtesy break. Mine are buzzing big time. I take this opportunity to whisper the details of the plan to Beth. She nods and follows me to an opening closer to Jasper, her friend trailing in a silent cloud of confusion. The club is filled to capacity: bodies everywhere. When the next song starts, I smash into Beth. She drops her big black purse in front of where Jasper's bobbing his head to the erratic beat.

Her friend yells, "Beth, your bag!" just as someone kicks it and her belongings go flying.

While I'm acting oblivious and dance-shoving her friend away, I send Jasper a telepathic message: *Come on. Be a gentleman. Help the lady out.*

Sure enough, Jasper taps Beth on the shoulder to get her attention, then points to the floor, where her purse and all its innards are being scattered all over the dance floor. They both stoop to collect the makeup and pens and Certs, and even from ten feet (and fifteen bodies) away I believe I detect a spark zapping between the two.

When the song wraps up, Beth joins us, all smiles. Her friend, who undoubtedly thinks I'm a raging idiot, shouts over the din, "This band is crap. Let's blow," and starts heading for the exit.

Oh no. I just need a little more time. I grab Beth's arm. "Jasper doesn't like the band either. Tell me where you're going next and I'll put the word out."

"The Crow's Nest." Her violet lips curve into a smile. "Thanks."

The band blasts into another set. "E-mail me later and let me know how it goes."

"'Kay."

I scan the room for Jasper but pause when I spot Derek. He's standing at a cocktail table with Brian, bobbing his head to the beat. I wonder if he's a good dancer. I wonder if he's a good kisser.

Whoa, girl.

I force myself to tear my eyes from Derek and finally spot Jasper and his friend at the bar. I drift up to Jasper and say nonchalantly, "Oh, hey, again." Whew! Being Miss Match is hard work. I'm totally out of breath.

He takes a swig of his drink. "Hey."

"This band sucks, huh?"

He chuckles. "Yeah, pretty weak."

"I hear the Mayhem Festival's gonna be killer this year."

"Halloween, right?"

"Mmm-hmm. It's supposed to be our generation's Woodstock or Lollapalooza or whatever." I turn to the bartender. "Can I get a Diet Coke?"

"So did ya ever find your friend?" Jasper scratches behind his ear. "She was dancing over by us a minute ago."

"Oh, Beth? Yeah. But she blazed. I guess the Crow's Nest is where it's at tonight." I smile around Jasper's shoulder at his friend. "You guys going?"

They exchange glances. Jasper shrugs. "Guess so."

"Well, tell Beth hi for me. I've got to get home. Lame-ass curfew." They nod understandingly.

"Hey, here's your Diet Coke!" the bartender hollers at me.

I hold up my pointer finger in the *just a sec* gesture and then turn back to the guys. "Well, see ya around."

"See ya."

I slap a five on the bar and scurry over to the dance floor. Yas is going to think aliens abducted me.

"Where've you been, girl?" she asks.

I join her and start swinging my hips around in a way I hope looks somewhat sexy. Actually, I'm happy if I simply don't look ridiculous. "Working, believe it or not."

"Oh, I believe it." She rolls her dark kohl-lined eyes. "Did you see Derek? He's here." She puts her hands behind her head, wriggles down to a semi-crouching position, then pops up. It feels like the whole club is staring at us. Well, *her*, anyway. I'm just mesmerizing by association.

"Yeah, and Brian's here too."

She pauses. "Are you working *right this very minute?*"

Brian and Derek are where I last saw them. I catch Brian's eye and curl my finger at him to say, *Come hither*. He ducks his head a little, saying something to Derek. A minute later they're heading right for us.

"What are you up to, Miss Match?" Yas asks, silently mouthing the last part.

Brian's definitely checking out Yas's body as she twists and shimmies. He dances closer to her, looking like a hybrid between

Will Ferrell and the Easter Bunny.

Derek, on the other hand, is actually a good dancer. Not Justin Timberlake good, but he can definitely hold his own in a Utah dance club. Taking a quick break from being the matchmaker, I allow myself to have some fun. I can totally see why Yasmin is so into the club scene. You can get lost in the music, the energy—the hot guy dancing with you.

Even though I have a smile plastered on my face, depression is setting in. The next time Derek will be dancing will be with Maddie. She's going to look drop-dead gorgeous, and he won't be able to take those amazing blue eyes off her. They'll probably kiss that night. Maybe more.

Oh my God, I feel sick! "I'll be right back," I announce to no one in particular. I run to the bathroom and push my way to the mirror. Some girl says, "Watch it, loser." But I don't even give her the satisfaction of a retort.

I stare at my reflection. What's gotten into me?

Get a grip, Sasha.

I take a deep breath and try to smooth the static out of my hair. I've got to get back out there and be Miss Match. I've got to make sure Brian asks Yasmin to homecoming. There's no time to feel sorry for myself. There's no time to get all hot and bothered over a guy who obviously isn't the least bit interested in me.

But there *is* time to go to the bathroom. I mean, I *am* in the ladies' room already.

When I come out of the stall, Yas is waiting by the sinks, grinning from ear to ear. "Guess what!" She slips her lip gloss into her pocket.

"What?"

She starts hopping up and down with excitement, though if someone were to walk in just now, they might assume she has to pee really, really bad. "I'm going to homecoming!"

"That's great!" I hug her, thankful for the diversion. Incidentally, being Miss Match helps keep my mind off my personal romances. Or lack thereof. "With who?"

"Brian Goldman. As if you didn't already know."

I widen my eyes, hoping to look all innocent. "How would I know?"

"Give me a break, Sasha," she whispers. "I saw the little hole in his back where you shot your Cupid arrow."

"He *wanted* to ask you, hon. He just needed to be reassured. So how'd he do it?"

"He just swung me around a time or two and asked me outright. Not nearly as romantic as when Derek asked your sis, but hey. Got the job done."

"That's fabulous, girl."

She studies my reflection in the mirror for what seems like a week. "Why don't you come with us?" she asks.

"What do you mean?"

"You know. Come to homecoming with Brian and me. We're all friends."

I force a smile and fiddle with the gold heart charm she gave me for my b-day. "That's really sweet of you, but I think I'll pass this time."

She shrugs. "Okay, well, let me know if you change your mind."

"Will do."

We turn to leave. "Sasha?"

"Mmm?"

"Will you go shopping with me? You know, to get my dress?"

I squeeze her hand. "Of course! What are best friends for?"

When we get back to the dance floor, Derek and Brian are right where we left them. Only now there are a couple of other chicks closing in on them, hungry looks in their heavily made-up eyes. Yas grabs my arm and pulls me through the sea of dancers, emerging up-close-and-personal with her homecoming date. He takes her by the shoulders and whisks her away, leaving me to fend for myself.

"You've been busy tonight," Derek says. He doesn't miss a beat, dancing closer to me, cutting off the other girls.

I shrug, hoping to look nonchalant. Hoping to appear completely unfazed by the heat radiating from his amazing body. Fact is, as Miss Match I have had a heckuva lot on my agenda tonight. But the one thing that stands out—the one thing that's etched in my mind—is dancing so close to Derek.

Mom, Maddie, and I are at Café Rio. Ceiling fans whir overhead, and servers in white ruffled blouses dart around, balancing trays of margaritas and tamales. Black and white photos of cactuses and old pickups—much like Derek's—adorn the red and green wall behind us. I dunk a blue tortilla chip in the salsa and chomp it loudly, the crispiness, saltiness, and spiciness mingling on my tongue.

Mom put this little Sunday dinner together so Maddie and I could meet Holden properly. As soon as he saunters through the door, Mom's face lights up.

Holden slides into the booth next to Mom and pecks her bright pink cheek. "Sorry I'm late, ladies. So, you must be Maddie," he says, beaming at my sister. Then he looks at me and does a double take.

I fill in the blank for him. "Sasha."

A huge smile appears on his handsome face, and I realize he recognizes me. "You!"

Mom sets her strawberry margarita on the table. "You know each other?"

The waitress pauses at our table to take Holden's drink order. "I'll have a margarita on the rocks," he tells her. When she leaves, he turns to Mom. "Sasha's the whole reason I called you. She approached me at Starbucks and gave me your business card. She insisted I give you a call."

"Way to go!" This is from Maddie, of course.

Mom laughs and shakes her head. "I should have known."

Later that night, there's a knock on my bedroom door. I look up from my American History textbook. "Come in."

Mom walks in and sits at the foot of my bed. She's wearing flannel pajama pants, but her makeup and jewelry are still on. "Where'd you get that sweatshirt?" she asks. "Are you wanting to go to A&M or something?"

"Naw. A friend loaned it to me." I know I should give it back to Derek, but it's so cozy, and wearing it really boosts my spirits. I'd never wear it to school or out in public, though. I'd be mortified if Derek spotted me parading around in his sweatshirt. I figure I'm safe as long as I just lounge around in it in the privacy of my own home.

"So, you played matchmaker for Holden and me?"

I nod. "I thought he looked like your type. And you'd seemed lonely lately. Why should Dad have all the fun?"

A big smile fills her eyes. "Just wait till that baby is born. He'll be having so much fun he won't know what hit him." She laughs and fluffs one of my pillows (unlike Derek, I have lots of them). "Holden and I get along very well. You're a natural."

"That's why I do it. I love to see people get together. It makes me happy."

"Thanks for making me happy, Sasha."

"You're welcome."

"Now I want to do something for you." Mom stands. "Be right back."

A few minutes later Mom is back in my room, handing me an envelope. "I've wanted to do this for quite a while. A big sale came through, and I finally can."

I peek in the envelope. There's a fat stack of green bills inside. "Wow, Mom. Are you sure?"

She kisses me on my forehead. "I'll take you to get your license first thing in the morning. Now call your father and tell him to take you car shopping."

I laugh, that sweet-sixteen giddiness coming back to me. "Yes, ma'am!"

Twelve

Here is a picture of Jasper.

Sorry it took so long. I've had the flu. Being
sick sucks.

He did show up at the Crow's Nest and we talked
for a bit. What's your next plan?

Beth

Subj: Re: Took a Pic
Date: October 7, 11:05 PM Mountain Standard Time
From: MissMatch@MissMatch4Hire.com
To: Goth1900@kmail.com

Beth,

The photo is great. I just wanted it to put with your poem as kind of a little "Ode to Jasper" project I'm putting together on your behalf. I have a feeling it'll secure a Mayhem Fest date for you.

I'm glad you 2 got to hang out last weekend. I'll be in touch.

xoxo
M.M.

P.S. Maybe try to wear something a little less . . . black . . . once in awhile. Just for kicks. It will make Jasper notice you, and that would be a good thing.

You've got to be kidding me. My phone's going off! Right in the middle of my chemistry midterm.

Mr. Foley stomps down the aisle and gives me the look of death. I swear Derek's going to burst out laughing any second. This is so not funny, though.

"Miss Finnegan, what is the rule about cell phones in class?"

"I know, I know."

He holds out his hand. I give the caller ID a quick glance. Dad. Hasn't he ever heard of text-messaging? I open the phone and hold it out to Mr. Foley. "It's my father, Mr. Foley. Will you please tell him to stop calling me at school?"

He grabs my phone and snaps it shut. "I don't care if it's the president of the United States, Miss Finnegan. This behavior is unacceptable. You may leave now and take your cell phone with you. Your classmates are trying to take an exam, and it's not fair that they've been so rudely interrupted."

"I agree," I say, sinking into my chair. "I'm so sorry this happened. Look, my cell phone is powered down. And you can confiscate it for a whole week if you want to. But please don't make me leave. I'm not finished with my test." People are staring, but I don't care what they think.

Mr. Foley shakes his head. "I'm sorry, Miss Finnegan, but you've been warned. You're dismissed."

Crap! I stand up and chuck my phone into my backpack. Next, I place my half-finished exam on Mr. Foley's desk. *Please, Mr. Foley, have a heart and grade what I was able to finish.*

By the time I get out in the hall, I'm furious. Why can't I ever remember to turn the damn thing off while I'm in class? I dial Dad's work number, and the receptionist puts me through. "Hi, honey! How's your day going?"

"Well, I just had to leave my chemistry class when I wasn't finished with my midterm. If I'm lucky, I'll get a fifty percent."

"I'm sorry to hear that, Sasha. I know how much your grades mean to you."

"No one even calls me during school except for you. And since you've called me twice during the same class, the teacher kicked me out." I make a sound like a deflating balloon and slide down a random locker to the floor. I'm sure I'll have attractive specks of dirt all over my black pants, but I've got bigger things to worry about. "Not that I'm blaming you. It's my own fault. It's just . . ."

"I really am sorry. Do you want me to call the school, talk to somebody about it?"

"No, that's okay. So what do you want, anyway?" This better be important.

"I got your message. I take it you want to look at some cars?"

"Oh. Yeah. I got my driver's license," I say, amazed how a little piece of plastic could make me feel so grown up. "I plan on selling my Vespa—Mom said Pearl's assistant really wants it—and Mom gave me some money last night. Plus, I have a little money saved up. So if you hold up to your promise, the way I figure it . . ."

"It's time to get you a car." After a brief pause, he says, "That sounds great. I'll pick you up at five thirty."

"Cool."

I hang up and walk by the chemistry room, peeking in. Derek catches my eye and waggles his finger at me like *naughty, naughty*. Punk.

I flip him off but can't help smiling. How is it that Derek can always lift my spirits?

"No Valerie?" I say, plopping into the shotgun seat of Dad's white Explorer. This is the first time his SUV has been in the driveway since the divorce was finalized. Since I backed into Mrs. Woosely's car, come to think of it.

"No, she had some things to take care of.

She did mention wanting to take you girls shopping after school tomorrow, though."

The cheapskate who talked Dad into getting me a scooter instead of a car wants to take us shopping? "Like to buy us stuff? You've got to be kidding me." Oops, did I say that out loud?

Dad chuckles and backs out of the driveway. "I'm not joking."

"Did you already talk to Maddie?"

"She's all over it."

"Figures." I sigh. "Okay, I'm in." I so don't want to go shopping. Helping Yas hunt down the perfect homecoming gown Sunday afternoon totally burned me out. It took four hours and six different stores to find a knee-length red strapless number she liked well enough. I almost missed dinner with Mom's new boyfriend! And it's not like she didn't look amazing in every single one she tried on. Sheesh!

Dad drives to Broadway Street and turns right, where there's a jungle of used-car lots. "Eeny meeny miny mo," I chant under my breath.

"Let's give this one a go." Dad turns into a lot with enormous witch and pumpkin blow-up things beckoning from the street.

I crane my neck to take in the offerings at Bernie's Autos. Almost immediately, I spot an adorable red Jeep with a tan top. My heart skips a beat. The writing on the windshield reads *What a deal!* but it might as well read *Sasha's*. I unbuckle my seat belt and thrust open the door, desperate to get a closer look. I deftly dodge the burly sales-man (with the unfortunate comb-over) and practically run across the lot.

My dad, who's now within earshot, clears his throat the way he does when he's getting down to business. "So, how does it run?" he asks.

"Like a champ," the salesman says. "I can work out a really nice deal for you today, sir. Looks like your daughter really likes it."

I peek in the windows. Tan seats, looks clean. Next, I walk around to the back. A few scratches on the bumper; nothing major, though.

"What kind of deal?" Dad asks.

The salesman answers, but it's too quiet for me to hear from where I'm standing.

Dad nods, a contemplative look on his face. "Okay, can we take it for a test drive?"

"Sure! Let me just get the key and the license plate. Be back in a jiffy." Obviously pleased, the salesman jogs to the trailer office.

While we're waiting, I untie the balloons on the Jeep's windshield wipers and set them free. Only they're helium-challenged, so they kind of bob around in the air rather pitifully and eventually land by Dad's loafers.

"Okay, let's take this baby for a spin!" the salesman says, kicking the balloons out of his way. He slaps the license plate on the back and jangles the keys, a goofy grin on his clean-shaven face.

"We'd rather just the two of us go. You understand." Dad says this in a way that leaves no room for arguing. After a moment of hesitation the salesman relents and drops the keys into Dad's open palm.

"Thanks!" I say, and jump behind the wheel.

We creep through the parking lot and onto Broadway, my stick-shift abilities obviously in need of some major help. Shoot! Killed it.

"It will come with time," Dad says, tightening his seat belt.

Feeling encouraged, I start it up again and cruise through a yellow light. Driving around town for about fifteen minutes I start getting the hang of the whole gas-clutch-brake-clutch rhythm. Whenever I mess up, the Jeep hiccups or stalls to rub it in my face.

"Do you like the way it drives?" Dad asks, poking around into the glove compartment.

"I guess so. Not like I have much to compare it to, though. You want to drive?"

I veer off into a neighborhood, and Dad and I perform a seat swap at the first stop sign we come to. After driving around for about five minutes he says, "It seems to be okay, but I think we should have a mechanic look at it. You know, just to see if there's anything wrong with it."

"Yeah, that's a good idea." Then I think of something. "Hey! I know a guy who's great with cars. Maybe he could take a look. Mind if I take the wheel?"

The Jeep's tires sputter gravel up the Urbans' driveway. An array of emotions are dancing in me, fighting over which one gets to lead. I really love this Jeep and hope it's in good shape and we can afford it and everything. I can totally picture myself buzzing around in this baby, the top off when it's warm and the four-wheel drive helping me plow through the snow in the winter.

And, okay, my romantic side is really

excited to see Derek. Not that I want to admit it, even to myself.

"Lookie there! Now that's a great old truck," Dad says, taking in Derek's Chevy, which is parked perfectly straight in the driveway.

I toot the horn in a friendly *honk-honk*, and the airy drapes on the front window flutter in response. A minute later the front door swings open and Derek comes jogging out in a flannel shirt and jeans. His eyes are so bright, and he's got an enormous, goofy-looking grin on his face.

Why is he so happy? Could it be he's glad to see me?

"Sorry, Sasha. I didn't recognize you without your helmet."

I roll my eyes, but I can't help giggling a little. After I introduce them, Dad asks, "So, you're the young man taking Maddie to homecoming?"

Derek's smile grows, and I think his chest even puffs up a bit.

Oh.

So *that's* why he's in such a great mood. It must be sinking in that he's successfully won a big date—second only to prom—with Maddie Finnegan.

"If you're not too busy, I was wondering if you can take a look at this Jeep? We're taking it for a test run and want to know if it's a lemon or if it's in good shape."

Derek nods and heads over to the garage. He punches in a code and as the door lifts says, "Well, I can't guarantee it's not a lemon, but I can certainly let you know if I detect anything suspicious or wrong with it." Armed with his trusty tool box, he lifts the hood.

As Derek twists and prods various gizmos under the hood, Dad chats him up like he's his future son-in-law or something. I lose myself in the fantasy that he's my boyfriend (*not* Maddie's homecoming date) and how happy I am that he and my dad are getting along so swimmingly.

At one point Derek looks at me and grins, a smudge of grease on his cheek. Instinctively, I take a Kleenex out of my purse and wipe his cheek clean. When his eyes widen and his face flushes, I realize I've crossed back into reality. They do a few more tests and talk about car parts, but I'm totally lost and realize trying to keep up is a futile effort. So I just stand here, grinning like a fool.

Because I am a fool.

Why am I torturing myself like this?

I mean, nothing's changed. Derek's still going with my sis to the homecoming dance. They're both totally excited to be going together. These stupid fantasies about kisses and relationships with Derek are just wreaking havoc with my heart.

Dad shakes Derek's hand. "Well, Derek, thanks again for taking a look."

"No problem. My pleasure." Derek waves as I crawl into the driver's seat and turn on the ignition. I glance at him in my rearview mirror before turning up the street, and I unceremoniously stall the engine.

"You'll get the hang of it!" Derek hollers. He shakes his head, chuckling. I bite my lower lip and start up the Jeep again, determined to make it out of his sight without any more embarrassing mishaps.

When we get back to the car dealership, my dad says, "Sasha, I thought you'd be more excited. What's the matter?"

I sigh, wondering if I should admit what's gnawing at me. No, not about Derek. I guess I'm glad he's so excited about going to the homecoming dance with Maddie. What I'm thinking about is how I've covered up the whole accident with Mrs. Woosely. If I admit that I was responsible for a fender-bender in his SUV and that I kept it a big secret from him and Mom, there's a chance he'll be so mad he won't let me get the Jeep. But I'd feel really guilty driving around in it without first coming clean. If he changes his mind, I can't blame the guy. It's a risk I've got to take.

"I have something I want to tell you," I say softly, looking straight ahead. In my peripheral vision I can see that Dad's stopped cleaning his glasses and is giving me his full attention. The light at Broadway and Main turns red. *Clutch in, brake in, eaaaaasy does it.* "Remember that day I was shooting hoops and you and Mom were inside and I came in a lot earlier than you expected and you asked if I'd had any problems moving your truck and—"

"Yes. I remember."

Downshift.

"Well, I actually had a teensy-weensy fender-bender with Mrs. Woosely." I go on to explain exactly what happened and how we made arrangements to have me pay her back for the repairs, and though Dad is listening intently, I can't read his mood-ometer.

Slowly, I pull into the car lot, park by the office, and hand Dad the keys. He stares down at them, tosses them up and down a few times, and then gets out.

⭐

"The red one in the back row?" Yas asks me the next afternoon.

I nod and break into a smile. "Yep, that adorable Jeep is all mine."

She twirls her combo and opens her locker. "So I take it all the purple Jeeps were taken?"

"Yeah, well, Dad and I scoured the entire state for one, but sadly, the only one we found belonged to a crazy Utah Jazz fan who wasn't about to surrender it."

"Aren't *all* Jazz fans crazy?" She winks and starts stacking her books in her locker. "Well, I have to say, being a car owner suits you. Your hair looks amazing."

Pleased that she noticed I say, "Thanks. Well, I'd offer to take you for a spin, but Valerie is taking Maddie and me shopping."

"Are you serious?" she asks, whipping around.

"Yeah, wish me luck."

Yas just laughs. "I can't wait to hear all about it."

A few minutes later Maddie and I meet in the teacher parking lot to wait for Valerie to pick us up. Twenty more minutes pass before her shiny Lexus glides up to the curb. She waves at us as if she hasn't seen us for years.

"Girls, I'm delighted you could make it. This is going to be so much fun!" Maddie takes shotgun and I buckle up in back. Valerie's SUV smells like gardenias, which I trace to a flower-shaped air freshener on the gearshift. She turns off the KSL Radio talk show and waits while the elderly choir director shuffles across the faded remains of a crosswalk.

"So, Valerie, what are we shopping for?" I ask.

Maddie whips around and rolls her eyes at me. "You don't have to always have a goal in mind, Sasha. Shopping is more about bonding than finding and purchasing something in particular." She settles back down in her seat. "Right, Val?"

Val? Don't tell me Maddie is already bonding with the woman who broke up our parents' marriage, our future stepmother, the human incubator of our hopefully human half-brother or -sister.

Valerie peels out of the parking lot and eventually takes I-15 southbound. "You're right, Maddie. But today I do happen to have something very specific in mind. I think you'll be pleasantly surprised."

I cross my arms over my chest and lean back, staring out the window. The leaves have already turned red, orange, and yellow, and if this wind sticks around, the branches will be stark naked in no time. "So, if it's a surprise, does that mean we have to wait and see what you've got in mind?" Maddie asks.

Valerie pats Maddie's knee. "You'll see soon enough."

We pass the Murray city-limit sign, and I bolt upright. "Are we in a hurry, Valerie?"

"Not really."

"Do you think you could stop at that school right there? I just have to drop something off real fast."

"Sure."

The shiny Lexus pulls up to the front of Murray High School. I grab my backpack and jump out before Maddie can interrogate me.

Once inside, the office is simple to find. I take Beth's poem and photo out of my backpack. I've put them together in what I hope is an artistic way. In the research I've done, artist types are especially moved by things like poems and pictures. Hopefully Jasper will appreciate this.

The rosy-cheeked office lady glances up from her computer screen when I walk in. "Hi," I say. "I need to have this folder delivered to one of your students tomorrow. It's important."

She nods to a big wooden box on the wall. "If you just set it in there, I'll be sure it's delivered tomorrow morning."

"Thanks."

I run back to Valerie's SUV, and we're off for whatever shopping adventure she has planned for us.

Ten minutes later she pulls into a parking spot by a small strip mall, and we pile out. She links elbows with us and escorts us to the sidewalk and toward a big sign that reads ANNABELLE'S WEDDING SHOPPE in curlicue lettering. My sneakers get heavier and more sluggish with every step. I try to catch Maddie's eye, but she's facing straight ahead, looking as terror-stricken as I feel.

Valerie opens the door, but I don't budge. "What's going on?"

Thirteen

"I want you two to be my bridesmaids," Valerie says as she pushes through the wedding-store door. A little silver bell chimes daintily.

"You can't just spring this on us," I say through clenched teeth. "You're supposed to *ask* us." That's the way they do it in wedding-themed movies, anyhow.

Valerie's forehead furrows, and her lips form a thin, flat line across her flushed face. "You're right, Sasha." She takes our hands, and for a scary moment it feels like she's going to play ring-around-the-rosy with us. "Your father and I decided it would make our special day even more special if the two of you would be bridesmaids. Will you do us that honor, girls?"

I don't know about Maddie, but I'd rather jump into the Great Salt Lake. With open cuts all over my body. I take my hand back and place it firmly on my hip.

A white-haired woman in a pink Chanel-like suit stops vacuuming the shiny mauve carpet and hustles to the entryway. She looks like a sparrow with a freakishly large bosom. "I'm sorry; I didn't hear you come in," she says, reaching out to ring the bell on the door. "I should get a louder one of these, I suppose." She giggles and then chirps, "Ms. Kensington, so delightful to see you again. And these must be the bridesmaids. Mercy, me! They're every bit as beautiful as you described." It's hard to look beautiful when you're fuming.

"Well, actually, they haven't answered yet." Valerie blinks a few times and then asks, "Well, ladies? What do you think?"

"Will you excuse us?" I grab Maddie's arm and yank her outside.

"Can you believe it?" Maddie asks. There's a wistful look in her eyes, like she's not only okay with this, but actually excited about it.

"You *want* to be a bridesmaid for Valerie?" I ask, dumbfounded.

She spins around to look at the gaudy bridal gown in the window. "I guess it depends on what the dresses look like."

I roll my eyes. "Why couldn't Dad have warned us?"

"He's not *that* bad," Maddie says, shrugging. "He tries."

My mouth suddenly dry, I open my purse and feel around for my mints. My fingers skim my red plastic heart key chain. The one Dad bought me yesterday to put my new Jeep key on. The Jeep that Dad paid well over fifty percent for when he saw how badly I wanted it. Which was really sweet and, yes, generous—especially taking into account the money-gobbling wedding and baby on the horizon.

I have to admit, Dad has been making an effort lately. Kinda weird, but I think we might be talking and hanging out more than when he lived at home. "Come on, Maddie."

Back in the bridal shop Valerie is sitting on a plush couch-bench thingy, her legs crossed, quite prim and ladylike, sipping champagne out of a delicate flute. "Is everything okay?" she asks.

"You shouldn't be drinking, what with

being pregnant and everything," I mutter under my breath.

Valerie giggles. "It's nonalcoholic, Sasha. This *is* Utah, after all."

The saleslady jogs over, her glasses slipping down her nose. "Your dresses are hanging in the big dressing room in the back, girls. Just go through this curtain and you'll see them. After you're dressed, come out so I can see what needs to be nipped and tucked."

Is she referring to the dress or my body?

We close the dressing-room door and strip. I catch Maddie's reflection in the full-length mirror. She's so long and lean, everything I've ever wanted my own body to be. She slips into her size-four dress—a deep maroon sheath with a plunging neckline and a slit that hits just above the knee. I hate to admit it, but it's lovely. Stunning, even. Especially when modeled by Maddie Finnegan.

"Hurry up, Sasha. I want to go home and see what Derek has planned for Saturday night."

Saturday night. Homecoming. The big-deal social affair that I'm not going to be a part of. I take the size-eight gown off its hook and slip it over my head, the static electricity having a field day with my hair.

"Want me to zip it?" Maddie asks, and I nod.

It won't zip.

It. Won't. Zip.

After another attempt she says, "Well, let's just go out now. I'm sure the lady can make it work."

My nose is stinging. *Don't cry, Sasha.* It's really no big deal. It's just a freaking dress, for God's sake.

Maddie parades out and is treated to a chorus of oohs and aahs. "It's simply gorgeous," Valerie coos.

While I watch from behind the curtain, the saleslady sticks some pins in Maddie's dress, marking where it needs to be taken in. "We could have gone with a size two for you, dear."

Then I walk out.

"Oh, dear," the shop lady says, frowning as she tugs the dress at my waist. "Well, look on the bright side. We still have time to order a size ten. Or maybe we should go with a twelve, just to be safe."

Valerie places her empty champagne glass on a little Victorian table. "That color looks great on you, Sasha."

Just kill me now.

After school I let Beth know that the poem and picture were delivered to her school and that Jasper should have received them sometime this morning. I hope that goes well. It worked wonders when I was helping a freshman guy named Simon get the attention of the sophomore girl he was crushing on last April.

Yasmin bursts into my room, two Styrofoam cups in hand. "They're having happy hour at the local Sonic," she announces, setting the drinks on my desk. "Thought you might like a cherry limeade, you know, to cheer you up."

I frown. "I don't need cheering up."

"Whatever." She kerplops onto my bed. "So, are we going to the big football game tonight? I hear Harrison might actually give us some competition this year. Wouldn't that be something?"

"Definitely front-page news."

"Instead of the president's favorite salad

dressing? Whatever are we going to do? We'll have to risk everything and choose our *own* favorite dressing!"

Okay, so that came from left field. But anyway it got me laughing. Leave it to Yas.

"There, that's better." Yas passes me my cherry limeade, and as soon as I can control myself (I don't want it coming out my nose, after all), I take a hearty swig. "So what's wrong, girl? You can tell me."

I close my laptop and curl my knees up to my chest. "Where do I start?"

"Start at the very beginning and don't stop till you've vented your heart out. I'm all yours. That is, until six. I need at least an hour to get ready for the game, you know." She smiles at me and then makes herself comfy on the pillows.

"Well, first of all, Dad's getting married."

Yasmin's mouth drops open. "To his skanky boss?"

"Well, she's not as skanky as I thought she was. But yeah, that's her. And get this. They're pregnant."

I can tell Yas is trying not to laugh. She snorts instead. "Wow, that's . . . interesting."

"Maddie and I have to be bridesmaids."

Yas shifts her lips from side to side. "That could be fun, I guess. If the dresses aren't too hideous. I was a junior bridesmaid at my cousin's wedding, and I had to wear this floofy pink and white thing that looked more like a poodle costume than a dress."

"Actually, the dresses aren't bad. I just couldn't get into mine. They're having to order a bigger size."

"That's cool."

Hel-*lo*? Does she have her earbuds in or something? I sit up. "That's *not* cool, Yas. It means, it means . . ." Despite my fanatical blinking, tears spill down my cheeks. I've been holding them in since yesterday, and for some reason they choose this very moment to let loose.

While we were back in the bridal store's dressing room, Maddie did her best to downplay the fact that my dress wouldn't even zip. But somehow having a size-four—scratch that, size-*two*—person tell me that the dress was *made* for curvy bodies like mine . . . well, it just kinda sucked. But I have to give the girl props. I mean, she could've been a real jerk about it, you know?

Yas hugs me. "Don't let a stupid bridesmaid gown get you down, Sasha. The sizes are all screwed up on fancy dresses like that, anyway. Sweetie, you're adorable. And more than that, you're totally smart and fun to be with."

I sniff. "If I'm so adorable and smart and fun to be with, why am I the only upperclassman at Snowcrest who doesn't have a date tomorrow night?"

"You're not the only one." Yas passes me a Kleenex. "I hear Kevin McGregor's dateless. But he's up for homecoming king, so he's just going stag."

Hmm, that's odd. I thought he would've asked another girl to homecoming, seeing as how his number-one choice was going with somebody else. He could've asked just about anyone.

"Gotta admire the guy," Yas continues, "even though he totally dissed me at that Ruffalo dude's party." She sits up straight. "Maybe you two should go together. We could go shopping and put together a fab last-minute outfit."

"Kevin going to homecoming with me? Now *that*, my dear, would be front-page news." I shake my head. "No way. After all, I did everything in my power to keep him away from my sister. I'm sure he has a vendetta against me." And with good reason, really.

"Why don't you just come with Brian and me? It'll be fun."

I shake my head again. "Thanks, Yas. But no thanks."

"Too bad Derek's going with your sister. He seems like a really cool guy. And you two go together so well."

I want to play it cool and completely ignore what she's just said, but curiosity gets the upper hand. "What do you mean?"

She shrugs. "You just seem to get along really well with Derek, that's all."

Aaaah! I know! And I really love being with him. But I can't admit that to her. I just can't! "Well, Derek and Maddie are going to have a blast together. They get along really well too, you know."

"I guess." After a silent spell she asks, "So what does Susan think of her ex getting hitched and being a daddy all over again?"

I shrug. "I don't think she's especially happy about it, but she's making do. Actually, she's got a bit of a love connection happening herself these days." I can't help but smile, thankful for the change of subject to something much easier for me to talk about.

"That guy at Starbucks?"

"Yup."

"I swear, Sasha, you're amazing at fixing people up." Yasmin grabs my *Teen People* and flips through it, rubbing her wrist on the Paris Hilton Just Me perfume sample.

"Thanks."

"So, let's get you changed out of this ol' sweatshirt—which is way too big, by the way—and go to the game already!"

"I think I'll pass. I have an appointment with Mom's jetted tub."

She hurls the magazine at me. "You suck."

I grab her wrist and sniff. "Yeah? Well, you stink."

Mom's out with Holden, and Maddie has already left for the football game in her little winterized cheerleader outfit. The house is so quiet it's annoying. I grab my iPod and plug it into the stereo. I ripped a bunch of new songs a while back but haven't had a chance to listen to them.

"I don't suck," I say out loud. "I'm just sick of all this school spirit. Tonight is a night for *me*. I'm not going to work; I'm not going to study. I'm not going to worry what people think or do or don't do. I'm just going to enjoy having the house to myself."

I drift into the kitchen and scoop some rocky road into a bowl. I take a bite and then toss the rest down the sink. If I'm going to fit into my bridesmaid dress, I've got to stop eating so much.

Mom's new bubble bath is calling my name. Ever since she started dating Holden, she's splurged on wonderful lotions and potions. She even got herself a manicure the other day. I run the water, watching the tub fill with fragrant, fluffy suds. After lighting a few candles I slip out of Derek's A&M sweatshirt and my jeans.

Before jumping into the tub I find myself standing in front of the mirror. Holding out my arms and slowly turning around, I take in every inch of my body. My skin is radiant in the candlelight, and I've never really paid much attention to it before, but my neck is long and elegant, like Audrey Hepburn's. My legs are long and curvaceous, and they appear strong rather than flabby. And my stomach? It's no washboard, but it's certainly a lot flatter than it was last summer. Could synchronized swimming be making this much of a difference? Or am I just now seeing—really *seeing*—my body for the first time?

As I ease myself into the warm, sudsy water, all the adages from magazine articles I've read dance in my mind: You must first love yourself before someone else can love you; a confident woman is a sexy woman; every makeover starts from within. I vow to myself to get rid of my negative self-image and start fresh. I'll stop comparing myself to my sister and Yas and every other skinnier, prettier, more popular girl in the universe.

"It's out of necessity," I croon along with Simone Sez, "that I'm kicking you to the curb. But there are no hard feelings, only hard cement . . ."

The phone rings. I'm so not answering it. Instead I add some more hot water and sing my heart out. About thirty minutes later it rings again. There are probably barnacles growing on my butt by now, so I lug myself out of the tub and pick up the phone.

"Hi, Sasha?" a familiar guy's voice asks.

"Yeah . . ."

"This is Derek."

I know this sounds hokey, but my heart skips a beat. And I'm suddenly all too aware that I'm buck naked and dripping wet.

"Oh, hey, Derek. Hang on a sec." I grab Mom's terrycloth robe—the one Dad gave her for Christmas last year—and wrap it around me. Why is Derek calling me, anyway? "Okay, I'm back. Oh, wait. Hang on again. I've gotta turn down my music."

I turn it off. "Okay, now I can hear you. So, what's up?"

"Is Maddie there?" I mentally slap my forehead. *Duh.* He's calling for Maddie, not me.

"She's at the football game. It's homecoming. She's a cheerleader, so she kinda has to be there. She does the best spirit fingers, you know." This I say matter-of-factly, like a news reporter.

He pauses. "Oh, right."

"If you hurry, you can still catch the second half. I'm sure they'll all go out afterward."

"I'll pass."

"Why, Derek," I say, doing my best Scarlett O'Hara impression, "I do declare— you've lost your school spirit. Whatever are we going to do?"

"Fiddle-dee-dee, school spirit. Who needs it?" he says, playing along. "So, why aren't *you* at the game?"

I look down at my bare feet. "I was going

to play a little one-on-one, but Shaquille stood me up, the chicken."

"Maybe I could sub in. Let me talk to my manager."

"Okay. Have your people get in touch with my people."

"Will do."

We hang up, and I realize I'm smiling. You know? Yasmin is right. Derek and I really do get along well. He might as well be wearing an I'M WITH MADDIE FINNEGAN T-shirt, but that's okay. While being just friends might have a bad rap, I'd rather that than nothing at all.

Then it hits me that Derek might very well be coming over here and I've got to get dressed. I tear through my closet looking for something to wear. Let's see . . . something athletic but stylish. Okay, this pair of baby-blue Adidas sweatpants will work, but none of my tops look good with them. Will Maddie have something that will work?

I fling open her closet and begin thumbing through her clothes. She really does have a killer wardrobe. Finally, I pick out a white polar fleece top and drape it over my arm. Out of the corner of my eye, I spot a light pink gown in the back of her closet. I take it out and hold it up to myself in her full-length mirror. It's so dreamy: a Gunne Sax strapless. The bodice has a tulle ruffle at the top, and a dainty black ribbon adorns the waist. The satin skirt is full with layers of tulle underneath and scattered rosettes at the hem. I'm not sure when she picked it up, but this has homecoming-queen wannabe written all over it.

The robe falls to my ankles, and I slip the pink cloud over my head. It's so airy I can hardly tell I'm wearing anything at all. I ease the zipper up halfway and then twirl around Maddie's room, admiring my reflection in her silk-flower-adorned full-length mirror.

I'm the prima ballerina, pirouetting across the stage, curtseying as the audience tosses long-stemmed roses at my pink satin slippers. I spin around again—

The doorbell rings.

I peek out the window and see a '66 Chevy in the driveway. Quickly, I peel the dress off and hang it up, placing it back where I found it. No doubt about it, my sister's going to look amazing in that dress tomorrow night.

"You think you can hold your own?" I ask, dribbling the basketball past Derek's truck, straight for the hoop above the garage door.

I toss a slow-motion layup, and the net swishes obediently.

"Not bad, Sasha. But if that's your best, I'm afraid this is going to be a rather quick and painful game." Derek's wearing a pair of cords, a sweater, and cowboy boots. Not exactly a licensed NBA uniform, but hey, he looks cute. He smiles and catches the ball.

"So, are you totally excited or what?" I ask, taking the elastic off my wrist and pulling my hair into a no-nonsense ponytail.

"About . . . ?" He takes a shot from mid-driveway and it ricochets off the rim.

"Homecoming. With Maddie." Hel-*lo*? What does he think I'm talking about? Our chem final? Our synch-swimming routine? I snag the rebound and dribble to three-point range.

"Oh yeah. I'm sure it'll be fine."

"Curb your enthusiasm, cowboy."

"So who are you going with?" he asks.

I bounce the ball a few times. "No one. I'm not really into that sort of thing." At least that's what everybody thinks, anyway. No one seems to notice that I'm miserable about not having a date to the big dance. But hey, there's always prom.

He stoops over, ready to guard me. "Are you warmed up yet? 'Cause I'm ready to kick your butt all over this court—er, driveway."

I can't help but laugh. "Bring it on!" I aim at the basket and let it fly. *Swish!*

Twenty minutes later we're both sweaty and giggly and having a great time. Come to find out, Derek can definitely hold his own on the driveway court.

The sun has long since sunk behind the Great Salt Lake, and the temperature's dropping. Which reminds me, I've still got to give him his sweatshirt. "Be right back," I say, and rush inside to fetch it.

"Here ya go. Sorry it's taken me so long to return it." I hold out the A&M sweatshirt. "Thanks for letting me borrow it."

He shakes his head. "You know what, Sasha? I have a hundred just like it. My parents went a little overboard when we went visiting colleges last summer. So keep it. If you want to."

I'm trying not to appear as happy as I feel right now. I've really come to love this sweatshirt, and now it's officially mine! Instead of just wearing it at home in my bedroom, I can wear it anytime, anywhere I want to! "Okay, thanks."

He spins the ball on his finger, just looking at me. Finally, he breaks the silence. "Sasha, can I be honest with you?"

My breath gets stuck somewhere in my throat. "Of course." He hands me the ball, and his fingers brush mine. I bounce it a couple of times and then rest it on my hip, giving him my full attention. Trying to concentrate on what he's about to say, and not how he looks so adorable with his hair all messy.

"It's about tomorrow night. I'm nervous to take your sister to the dance."

What, did I think he was going to profess his love for me? Did I think he was going to admit he'd chosen the wrong Finnegan sister? I slip into Miss Match mode, hiding my disappointment. "Did I ever tell you how much Maddie loved your homecoming invitation? It's got to be the most romantic one in history. Every girl at Snowcrest is jealous."

His lip twitches, like he's trying not to smile. "I keep hearing my mother's voice in my head, saying, 'Derek, look what you've gotten yourself into.' She used to say that a lot when I was a kid. That and, 'No, you cannot let Bob in the house. He'll sleep just fine out in the barn.'"

We laugh.

"Here." I pass him the ball, then direct him to the makeshift free-throw line, a ragged crack in the cement. I put my hand over his eyes so he can't see. His face feels warm to my touch. Is the rest of his body this warm? "Shoot," I say. "If you make it, you and Maddie are destined to be together. If you miss, you aren't."

He takes a deep breath, one I can feel as if it's my own. "Okay."

The ball arches from his fingertips and flies through the evening sky. It bounces off the backboard and lands in a pile of crispy leaves beside the driveway.

A miss. A bad miss, really.

"Well?" he asks when I take my hand off his eyes. His eyes search mine, as if whatever I have to say is going to change his life forever.

I touch my gold heart charm and give him my best Miss Match smile. "You made it, lover boy."

Fourteen

"Where is Jenny?" Maddie practically screams. "Derek's going to be here in twenty minutes to pick me up, and my hair's not done."

"Do you need help?" I ask, looking up from my *Seventeen* mag.

Maddie is pacing around my room in her strapless push-up bra and matching panties, both (as if I need to say) pink. "She told me she'd be here at six o'clock on the dot. And it's already seven minutes past. She's totally late! How can she be so *insensitive*?"

"Do you want me to do your hair?" I try again.

She stomps over to my mirror and shakes her head upside down, her beautiful auburn hair swishing this way and that. She whips back up, lets out a very unladylike "Argh!" and storms out of my room, huffing, "I guess I'll just go put on my dress now." As if actually being dressed before Derek gets here wasn't part of her master plan.

Five seconds later the ballerina princess formerly known as Maddie Finnegan is standing in my room again, hands on her hips. "Do you suppose you can stop reading that dumb magazine long enough to zip me up?"

She's just stressed, I tell myself, trying to calm myself down before I bite her pretty head right off. The zipper slides easily over her narrow, tanned back. "Are you positive you don't want me to do your hair?"

She turns around, a smile on her freshly lipsticked mouth, a look of delight splashed on her dewy face. "Sasha, that would be super!"

I roll my eyes and drag her into the bathroom, where I go to town with the straightening iron and the miniature white flowers she bought for the occasion. After I give her a hearty hairspray job, I step back to give her full view of the mirror. "What do you think?"

She flings her manicured hand onto her

heart and sighs. "Wow, Sasha. Who ever knew you were so good? I look . . . *perfect*."

I force myself to smile, knowing that in a mere five minutes Derek will be here to whisk her away. And I'll have hours and hours of Maddie-free peace.

But when the doorbell rings, I'm not as relieved as I thought I'd be. My stomach feels like it's tied in knots, and my hands go all sweaty.

"Where's the camera, Sasha?" Mom hollers. "We've got to get a photo of this!"

I grab the digital off my desk and bring it down to the foyer. When I see Derek in his black suit and white tie, his hair slicked back and his jaw clean-shaven, my stomach knots so tightly I can hardly breathe. Much less speak. I hand the camera to Mom.

"Now get close together, you two. Don't be shy," she says, playing the part of embarrassing parent with prowess.

Derek chuckles (hey, is he nervous?) and Maddie kinda rolls her eyes, but they do as Mom says. Derek and Maddie look like they just stepped out of *Teen Vogue*'s prom edition. I think I'm going to be sick. Seriously.

The camera clicks away, capturing the first moments of Maddie's senior homecoming. The happy couple exchanging corsage and bouton-niere, the happy couple quickly running out of happy couple poses. After about twelve years Mom stops photographing and says, "Well, you two, that should do it. Have a great time!" and disappears down the hallway, wrapping up her part of the homecoming preshow.

"Yeah, have a great time," I echo, infusing my voice with as much enthusiasm as I can muster.

"Oh my God!" Maddie says, poking around in her dainty beaded handbag. "I almost forgot my lipstick! I'll be right back, Derek." She skitters off in her high heels, leaving Derek and me alone.

"You look amazing, Derek. Really."

Is he blushing? "Er, thanks." He reaches up to his tie and loosens it a notch.

I'm not really sure what to say, and apparently he's speechless too. He's probably got visions of Maddie dancing around in his head. Maddie in her matching bra and panty set, perhaps. Ha! That would leave any guy speechless.

Then the strangest thing happens. Derek reaches out to me, pulls me in to his chest, and squeezes me tight. He's hugging me! His body feels so hard and muscular, just like I imagined he would feel. He rests his chin on the top of my head, and for a split second I'm in utter ecstasy. The stomach knots are gone, and in their place is a warm, happy feeling. I remind myself to breathe. Oh my God, he smells incredible. "What kind of cologne are you wearing?" I ask.

"Stetson."

Come again? Like that old man drugstore cologne? I must have a revealing look on my face, because Derek goes on to explain:

"It was a gift from my grandma." He smiles warmly. "I know you said Maddie likes that Polo one or whatever, but this is what my grandpa used to wear when he was alive, and it's a lot more me than some designer kind you get at department stores."

I nod, completely understanding.

"Oh!" Maddie says when she turns the corner and sees us standing here. Hugging. "Um, I'm back."

We let go of each other, but Derek's hand remains on my upper arm. Which is a good thing, because my knees are so weak I'm not sure I can stand on my own quite yet. "Thanks for everything, Sasha," he whispers in my ear, tickling it with his cinnamony breath.

He turns to my sister and sticks out his

elbow. "Ready to go?" She smiles at him and takes his arm as they walk out to his '66 Chevy.

I wave from the front porch, watching the truck disappear. Watching my sister take off with the guy I'm . . .

Oh, God . . . totally falling in love with.

The phone rings. "Sasha, can you get that?" Mom says, "I'm late for dinner with Holden."

"Sure." I plop onto my bed and pick up the phone mid-ring.

"Hey, is Maddie there?" an out-of-breath girl asks.

"Uh, nooooo. She's at homecoming."

"Oh, crapola! I was supposed to do her hair and I totally spaced it. I hope she's not pissed?"

"She's fine, Jenny. It all worked out in the end."

She exhales loudly. "Whew! Well, okay then. Laters."

"Laters," I say all air-headily, and then drop the phone on my bed.

When I look up, Mom's standing in my doorway, smirking. "One of Maddie's friends?"

I nod.

She walks in and sits beside me. "I really like that sweater," I say. "It brings out the green in your eyes."

"Thanks, honey." She takes my hand in hers. "Listen, are you okay?"

"What do you mean?"

"Do you want me to stay home? We can watch Audrey Hepburn movies and gorge on popcorn."

"Don't be silly, Mom. You've got a hot date. Go have fun with Holden."

"You sure?"

"Of course I'm sure. I've got tons of homework to do. Don't worry about me. I'm cool."

She stands and starts walking out of my room. When she gets to my door, she turns around and smiles. "You really are cool, you know that?"

I throw a pillow at her. "Get out of here. You're late!"

She laughs and finally heads out.

When I hear the hum of the garage door closing, my smile putters out, and my nose starts tingling. I grab as many of my pillows as I can hold and rock back and forth on my bed. How did I let myself fall for Derek Urban?!

★

Subj: Strangeness
Date: Oct. 10, 12:26 PM Mountain Standard Time
From: Goth1900@kmail.com
To: MissMatch@MissMatch4Hire.com

Jasper liked his photo and poem. When he came over to me in the caf to tell me so, I asked him to the Mayhem Fest. He said no. I asked why not and he said I'm just not his type. Whatever. The weird thing is, I've been so into Jasper I thought it would devastate me.

But for some strange reason, I'm cool with it. I mean, if I'm not his type, it's not like I'm going to change just for him, you know?

Then something really strange happened. This guy named Kyle overheard me and Jasper and told me I'm exactly his type and you know what? He seems really cool and he's not ugly or anything, and he was wearing a Stomick Ulsar concert T- shirt like I've got. I asked him if he wanted to go with me and he said yes! So I'm going with a guy I just met, but I really think we might be into each other.

Thanks for helping me with Jasper, even though it didn't end up like I thought it would. I consider

your service money well spent because without
you, I wouldn't have met Kyle. So thanks for that.

Take care,
Beth

Subj: Re: Strangeness
Date: Oct. 10, 10:02 PM Mountain Standard Time
From: MissMatch@MissMatch4Hire.com
To: Goth1900@kmail.com

Dearest Beth,

What a romantic story! I'm so glad everything
turned out so well for you. You're so right about
not changing yourself for a guy. It's just not worth
it to pretend to be someone you're not.

I've enjoyed working with you and I wish you and
Kyle the very best.

xoxo
Miss Match

I've closed Beth's file, flipped through
all my October magazines, called Dad and
offered to address wedding invitations (I'm
great at calligraphy, if I do say so myself),

scarfed an entire pint of Ben & Jerry's (screw it—they probably ordered me the size-twelve bridesmaid dress anyhow, and I'm really starting to embrace my body, curves and all), studied for our next chemistry test (Mr. Foley said he'd let us drop one test score this term, so as long as I get As on the rest of mine, I'm golden), and written a report on *Jane Eyre* that isn't even due till after winter break. I know, I'm a total geek. But I figure that as long as I keep busy, I'm not obsessing about what Maddie and Derek are up to at homecoming.

Only my shirt smells like Stetson, so it's impossible to get Derek out of my mind. I strip out of my Derek-scented clothes, put on my pajamas, and climb into bed.

Just as I'm getting comfy, the phone rings. I search for it in the folds of my sheets, finally finding it at ring number four.

"Hello?"

"Hey, Sasha. It's me." Maddie?

"What's up?" Why in the world is she calling me in the middle of her big date? "Did you get homecoming queen?"

"They're announcing it at ten thirty. But that's not why I'm calling. I need your help. It's an emergency!"

I sit up and flip on my bedside lamp. "What is it?"

"I broke my heel!"

I sink back into my pillow. "I'm sorry. That sucks."

"Well, *yeah*! So, anyway, I was thinking you could just grab your silver strappy sandals and bring them by the school? They're a bit too big, but it's better than hobbling around on a broken heel."

"Maddie, are you serious? I'm already in bed."

"You're in *bed*? Like sleeping?" she asks as if I just announced that I'm an alien and I'm taking her entire Depeche Mode CD collection to a lab on Mars.

"Besides, don't all the girls end up taking off their shoes to dance anyhow?" I try.

"That was junior high, Sasha. We're in high school now." Yeah, right. Well, maybe I haven't been to a school dance since junior high. But I'm so not bringing up that little morsel of humiliation.

"So, will you? I'll meet you in the gym parking lot. It'll just take a sec."

I bring my knees to my chest and sigh. I can't very well leave Maddie high and dry on her big night. "Okay, I'll do it. But make sure you're waiting right by the parking-lot doors, Maddie. I'm not coming in to find you."

"Oh, thank you so so so so so much! I owe you one, sis."

"Yeah, well, you owe me like two hundred and sixteen. But who's counting?" It takes me a moment to realize that she's already hung up.

I lug myself out of bed and throw on the clothes I was wearing before: jeans and a lavender cami with lacy straps and a coordinating cropped sweater. Derek's scent washes over me, and I get that fluttery feeling in the pit of my stomach all over again.

I suppose I could've just stayed in my pajamas, since Maddie's going to meet me in the parking lot. But knowing my luck I'd get pulled over by a policeman for being a horrible stick driver.

I blast my stereo, getting more pissed by the minute. Maddie has me get out of bed to bring her my shoes, and she isn't even here. I check my watch and make a mental agreement with myself that in two more minutes I'm outta here. Maddie can just go up and accept her homecoming-queen crown barefoot. Heck, didn't that one country singer chick accept her Grammy with no shoes on? Of course, she never won a Grammy—or any award, for that matter—again.

One more minute . . .

And then she appears, the lovely ballerina princess, illuminated by the fluorescent lights of the gym hallway.

I turn off my stereo and roll down the passenger-side window, letting in a chilly gust of autumn air. "Hurry *up*, Maddie."

She runs over, and I'm suddenly aware that she's got two fully functioning high-heel shoes on her feet. My cheeks heat up in anger.

"Your heel isn't broken!" I hiss as she pokes her rosy face in the Jeep.

Her smile deflates. "Oh yeah, that. Well, I actually just wanted to get you here. There's, uh, someone who wants you to be here."

"What are you *talking* about? I already told Yas I wouldn't third-wheel with her and Brian."

"Just park and come with me."

"Maddie, I'm not coming in. I already told you that. Now please pull your head out of my Jeep so I can go home."

She flings the door open and jumps into the front seat, her arms crossed across her

chest the way she does when Mom's not giving in to her every whim, like buying her
that three-hundred-dollar pair of boots she
saw in Neiman's.

"Get. Out."

"Not until you agree to go in. Just for a
second. Pleeeease?"

"Get. Out. NOW!"

Maddie shakes her head. One of the mini
white flowers in her hair comes loose and
flutters down onto the seat.

I try another tactic. "Listen, if you're
in here with me, you're going to miss the
homecoming royalty announcement. What
if you're voted queen and you're not there to
accept your crown or dance with the king?"

Her jaw drops just slightly before she
repositions it into a determined pout. "If I
miss it, I miss it."

Ominous clouds are gathering in the
midnight-black sky. Looks like rain.

I glance down at my watch. It's 10:24. If
the announcement is at 10:30, she's got to
hurry. "They'd have to give it to Kennedy if
you weren't there," I try.

Maddie doesn't move.

10:25.

"I'm not budging unless you come in

with me." She pulls down the visor mirror and sticks the flower back in her hair.

10:26.

She refreshes her lipstick and smacks her lips.

10:27.

My heart is beating like crazy. Is Maddie serious? Is she going to miss the homecoming-queen announcement over this? Whatever *this* is?

What *is* this, anyway? Why's she so resolute about me going inside?

10:28.

I slap my steering wheel. "Okay. Okay. I'll go. You win, Maddie."

She claps her hands together. "Super!"

I slip off my sneakers and put on my silver strappy sandals. Thank God I didn't come in my pajamas.

Fifteen

Maddie and I sprint through the gym hall-way and into the gym, where sure enough Mr. Green, the principal, is up on the stage, tapping the microphone. "Testing, one, two, three. Can you hear me?"

A lukewarm "yes" comes from someone on the dance floor. I duck behind Maddie, majorly embarrassed to be at my high school homecoming dance (a) in jeans and (b) dateless.

Maddie's totally in her element, though, and she sashays into the rainforest-decorated gymnasium with her flowery head held high. She's instantly swarmed by the Beautiful People, who are even more becoming than usual in their homecoming finery. I take a quick look around, but I don't see Derek. He's probably right here somewhere, hidden by the beefy football dudes.

I know I vowed to love myself, to be happy in my own skin. But I can't help wondering what it would be like to be Maddie, always the center of attention. I raise my eyes to the vine-covered ceiling, focusing on a cluster of black and white monkeys and next on some gigantic crepe-paper flowers.

Mr. Green's gravelly voice brings my attention back to earth. "It's my great pleasure to announce Snowcrest's homecoming queen." The band's drummer goes crazy until Mr. Green shoots him a glare and says, "That's enough!" out of the corner of his mouth.

The gym is eerily silent, the anticipation as thick as Mr. Green's glasses. Maddie and Kennedy exchange *may the best woman win* smiles, but they're probably thinking something more like, *I hope you wore waterproof mascara tonight, because you're gonna be bawling like a baby when I win, loo-zah.*

"Madelyn Finnegan!"

The room explodes into applause and whistles, hoots and cheers.

Yep, I'm doing it too. I might have always been jealous of my perfectly pretty, peppy, popular sister, but I'm her sister all the same. And this is her crowning moment. Literally. "Yay, Maddie!"

I have to give the girl credit. She is the proverbial homecoming queen. She squeals, covers her mouth with her quivering hands, blinks her long-lashed eyes in utter disbelief, and glides through the celebratory crowd dazed and glamorous.

As Maddie approaches the podium, Kennedy's face reddens, despite her unseasonably dark tan. Her mouth is all twitchy, like it can't figure out whether to smile or frown. Her left eye is twitching, too. Ah, well. At least her hair looks terrific.

Once on stage my sister pulls the mic down within reach and, like Reese Witherspoon accepting her Best Actress Oscar, pauses a moment to take it all in. "I honestly am at a loss for words," she says, all breathlessly. "This has got to be the best day of my life. I can't thank you enough for giving me this honor." Her bejeweled hand covers her heart. She takes another moment to adjust her shiny new crown, and then in her bubbly cheerleader voice says, "Thank you, Snowcrest!" followed by, I'm sorry to say, her famous spirit fingers.

With everybody cheering so loudly, it takes me a moment to realize someone's calling my name. I spin around and there's Derek, still in his dapper suit. Still smelling like old-man-drugstore-cologne heaven. Still so cute he makes my heart flip-flop.

"I didn't realize you were coming," he says, his dark blue eyes twinkling when the tinselly "rain" streamers catch the light just right.

"Me either." I nod to my sister, who's now standing to the side as Kevin comes up to give his homecoming-king speech. "She forced me. Probably so I could give her the full report about what people were saying about her while she was soaking up the royalty spotlight."

Derek laughs. "Well, she wears it well. The crown, that is."

"Yes, indeed."

Kevin escorts Maddie down from the stage, and the band breaks into a slow song. I smirk. "Ah, how sweet. The homecoming royalty dance."

The crowd parts like the Red Sea, giving the newly crowned couple plenty of room to sway back and forth in each other's arms. I watch them for a moment and then look closer.

What's going on?

Maddie lays her head on Kevin's chest and he brings her in closer. Something is swirling and whirling all around them. Not something I can see, exactly—but definitely something I can *feel*. It's like an aura or an orb or something. It's like . . .

Oh. My. God.

How could I have been so blind?

It's so *obvious!* Maddie and Kevin are totally. . . *perfect* together.

Derek is watching them too. His forehead is crinkled, but when he notices me staring at him, he smiles. Does he see it too?

Maddie and Kevin dance right up to us, and Maddie grabs my hand. She brings me in close, and Kevin steps back, giving us a sisterly minute. "Derek's the one who wanted you here, Sasha," she whispers in my ear. "He talked about you all night, nonstop."

I stare at her, flabbergasted.

"Ask him to dance already." And with that she gives me a little shove in Derek's direction and promptly reclaims her king. Others are coupling up and hitting the dance floor.

"Hi," I say, suddenly bashful around Derek.

"Hi."

We both speak at the exact same time, "Do you want to . . ." and start laughing.

He takes my hand. "Dance?"

We take a few steps out onto the dance floor, and he wraps his arms around my back. I reach around his neck and sway with him, with the music, with the sea of dancing bodies surrounding us. He pulls me in so close I can feel his boutonniere squishing against my shoulder.

I'm suddenly all too aware that I'm at homecoming with my sister's date, that this is the boutonniere she bought for him. That he's all dressed up and looking so amazingly hot not to be with me, but to be with Maddie.

Yet somehow, this just feels . . . so *right*. Like Maddie was just the person who got him here, and I was supposed to show up and be his date all along. Like it was planned or something. Like it was our . . . destiny.

Derek says, "You look like something's

bothering you. Is it my dancing? What are you thinking about?"

"Um, well . . . I . . ." Not my most eloquent moment by far. But thankfully Yas and Brian twirl over to us before I make more of a fool of myself.

"I'm so glad you decided to come, Sasha," Yasmin practically screams, her crimson dress fluttering around her even after the twirl ends. "And look at you!" She tugs me away from Derek and looks me up and down. "You're positively adorable. So *au courant* in jeans. I wish I would've thought of it! You'll definitely get Best Dressed in the homecoming section of the yearbook, Sasha."

I can't help but gloat. Yas thinks *I'm* au courant? Wow!

"Well, I'd better let you two get back to your dance," she says, grabbing Brian's hand. Brian's looking awfully sweaty and worn out already. But that's the deal you make when you take dancing-queen Yasmin to a school dance. That girl doesn't do breaks. Yas winks at me as she leads Brian to the center of the floor, and I wink back.

"So, Sasha, what's bothering you?" Derek asks when we're alone again. Well, as alone as two people can be on a crowded dance floor. "You're not getting off that easy."

"I guess I was just thinking about how weird this is. You and me dancing together. I mean, you're my sister's date, and I wasn't even coming, and . . ." I lift my head and search for Maddie. She's still burrowing into Kevin's chest, looking completely and utterly in love.

"And it all worked out, huh?" Derek finishes for me. He lifts my chin and gazes into my eyes.

I swear, my heart is beating so fast I think I might be having a heart attack. I stop dancing. Which is good, I guess, because the song's over. "You mean you don't mind?"

"No, it's okay that you're stepping on my toes. I'm sure it's just a temporary arrangement."

Positive that my face is bright red, I step back. "Oops. Sorry about that. It's just . . ."

"Yeeeees?"

God, why does he have to have such an incredible smile? Doesn't he know it's impossible for a girl to think straight when he's doing that?

The band launches into a hip-hoppy song, and a fresh group of kids hits the dance floor. Derek and I keep getting bumped, and I have to raise my voice in order to be heard. "You don't mind hanging out with me when you could be with Maddie?"

Derek takes my elbow and escorts me to the sanctuary of the punch bowl. I can't get a good look at his face, so I have no clue what he's thinking. He takes two cups, fills them halfway, and hands me one. "Let's grab a table," he says, as if I hadn't just asked him about Maddie. We make our way to an empty table by a huge cardboard tree. I stretch my neck to see him over the plastic birds-of-paradise centerpiece.

"You're not getting off that easy, Derek. Why are you hanging out with me when you could be with my sister?"

He gulps the last of his punch and sets the cup down on the blue foil–topped table. "Maddie's beautiful, and that's why I liked her at first."

Well, duh, I want to say. But I refrain.

"Then I got to know her, and I thought she was really nice. Pretty smart, too. She's finally getting algebra."

My heart drops all the way down to my silver strappy sandals. What was I thinking? Derek still likes Maddie. And from the sound of it he likes her a whole heckuva lot. I quaff the watered-down punch, hoping to hide any disappointment that might be registering on my face.

"Sasha?"

"Mmm?" I mumble from behind my cup.

"It's empty. You can put the cup down."

"Oh, right." I set the cup on the table, next to his, and shift my eyes to the dance floor. Everybody's having such a great time out there. Maddie's surrounded by her popular friends, Kevin beaming at her side. Yasmin is shaking her stuff as close to the band as possible, and Brian looks like he's doing a pretty decent job keeping up with her. Atta boy.

See, Miss Match? Look how happy everybody is. Love is a good thing.

It's just that it keeps happening for everybody else. Everybody but me.

Derek leans forward and puts his hand on mine. "Look at me."

Reluctantly, I do. Does he know I have a crush on him? Does he know I had that lapse of sanity, when I actually thought he might like me back?

"Listen, Sasha. I know I missed the basket last night," he says.

I bite my lower lip. "You do?"

"I missed it on purpose."

It takes a few beats for what Derek has just said to sink in. "I don't get it," I say.

"It wasn't Maddie I wanted."

Huh?

"It wasn't?" I ask when my mouth finally functions. Did someone turn up the thermostat or something? Why is it all of a sudden so freaking hot in here?

"Nope. Maddie's great and everything, but I'm afraid she's just . . . not my type."

"Not your type?" I say, sounding like a stupid parrot or something. "Maddie's *every* guy's type."

Derek shrugs. "I don't have chemistry with her. I have it with *you*."

Chemistry? Is he talking about the class? Or . . . actual *chemistry*? Like the magic when two people meet and fall in love? Does he think we have the connection that Holly and Paul have in *Breakfast at Tiffany's*, or Princess Ann and Joe in *Roman Holiday*? Oh, God. My heart is beating like crazy just thinking about it.

Derek tugs at his tie. "Is it hot in here, or what? How about we get some fresh air?" He scoots his chair out and stands up, offering me his hand. He escorts me to the eastern exit, turning heads in the process. Then he opens the door for me and does a little bow as I join him in the vacant hall. Despite the muffled music from the gym and the tinny sound of rain on the roof, everything is so still and quiet. I pray he can't hear my heart pounding.

I take a deep breath, conjuring up my Miss Match bravery. After all, being bashful might be demure and charming and all that good stuff, but it sure wastes a lot of time. And I want to get to the bottom of this, pronto. I take a step closer to him, close enough to detect a slight red punch-mustache on his upper lip. What would it be like to kiss that punch-mustache? *Mmmmm.*

Before I get too carried away with my little fantasy, I take another breath and blurt, "Are you saying you have a *thing* for me?" Argh. That didn't come out right. I sound like a freaking fourth-grader or something. But at least I got it out, right?

Derek nods. That's it. He *nods*.

He has a thing for me? Can this really be happening? Might as well double-check. You know, just to make sure.

"So let me get this straight—" Before I utter another word, Derek presses his finger on my lips and escorts me out the door into the student parking lot. We stand at the top of the stairs, the overhang sheltering us from the pouring rain. Derek sheds his jacket and drapes it over my shoulders. Then he wraps me in his arms and squeezes me against the warmth of his chest. His breath tickles the top of my head, little water puddles forming at our feet.

"Sasha, there's something you need to know about me."

I look up at him. His blue eyes are piercing into mine, demanding my full attention. I'm at once excited and nervous. Please don't say something horrible, Derek. I'm ready for something good to happen in my life. Something *really* good.

"I believe in making my own destiny."

"So get on with it, Tex," I whisper, slowly leading him into the rain.

He trails his finger along my jaw, making my knees shake. Then he tilts my chin up and presses his lips against mine. Oh, wow. Oh, WOW.

All the kisses I've watched over and over again on TV shows or in movies, all the articles I've read on what kisses really mean and what type should be given in specific situations, all the times I've spied on people making out in the halls and under the bleachers . . . none of it matters anymore.

Because I'm not Miss Match.

I'm the beautiful, smart, fun, and soaking-wet girl I've always wanted to be. I'm Sasha Finnegan.

I watch the '66 Chevy's headlights vanish down my street, and then I go (more like *float*) inside. It's not raining anymore, but I'm positively soaked.

"How was it, Sasha? Come tell me all about it!" Mom calls from the living room. I'm a little shocked she's still awake. I mean, it's gotta be almost one a.m.

"Hang on, let me put on some dry clothes first." I dash to my bedroom and slip into my pajama pants and the polar fleece top I wore yesterday when Derek and I played basketball—the one I borrowed from Maddie's closet. I make a mental note to ask her if I can have it. This thing has memories now. I grab an elastic off my dresser and pull my wet hair into a messy bun-ponytail thingy on the top of my head, pausing to take a look at my reflection.

I danced with Derek Urban. And not only did I dance with him, I kissed him.

Do I look any different? I lean closer to the mirror. We kissed so much, my lips are a bit swollen. But that's okay. I mean, they don't hurt. They actually feel really good. Come to think of it, my whole body feels really good. I smile at my reflection and then pad down the hall to the dimly lit living room.

Mom and Maddie are in their pajamas, cuddled up on the couch, and *Breakfast at Tiffany's* is on the TV. Mom looks up and pats the seat beside her. I plop down, and she wraps her arm around me.

"So was homecoming a blast, or what?" Maddie asks sleepily.

I nod and break into a huge grin. "Totally."

"Maddie tells me you got together with Derek?"

"Um, well . . ." I watch Holly Golightly jump out of the cab in the pouring rain and run down the dark New York street. "Yeah, I did. We had a really great time."

"So, are you going to go out with him sometime?" Maddie wants to know.

I laugh. "If he's lucky."

On the screen Holly runs right past Paul Varjak, her friend who's just professed his love for her. She's looking for her cat, a cat she refuses to name 'cause it doesn't belong to her and she doesn't belong to it. But that's where she's wrong. Holly and the cat *do* belong to each other, and what's more, they *need* each other.

Holly finally finds the cat in an alley, sheltered from the rain in a crate. She scoops up the wet fur-ball and goes to show Paul, who's waiting for her on the street. They hug, all three of them.

Mom, Maddie, and I sigh. Like we always do at that part.

But I've got a huge problem with the way it ends. Sure, it's romantic, but it's missing something. Something big.

Holly never names the cat. She never takes the risk. She never makes the commitment. She never gives herself to love.

Subj: Professional advice needed
Date: Oct. 11, 9:49 AM Mountain Standard Time
From: 66Chevy@kmail.com
To: MissMatch@MissMatch4Hire.com

Dear Miss Match,

I have a really big crush on this girl at my school. I got to dance with her at homecoming last night. We even made out in the rain. It was great.

The thing is, I think we really clicked. I'd really like to be in a relationship with her, besides just being lab partners. Do you think I have a chance?

Just call me . . . Tex

Subj: Re: Professional advice needed
Date: Oct. 11, 10:07 AM Mountain Standard Time
From: MissMatch@MissMatch4Hire.com
To: 66Chevy@kmail.com

Dear Tex,

Ask her out. She can't wait.

xoxo
M.M.

About the Author

Wendy Toliver lives in the Utah mountains with her three little boys, her husband, and other various wildlife. She graduated from Colorado State University with a BA in Speech Communication/Broadcast and has had a variety of jobs, from performing singing telegrams to working at an advertising agency. Now a soccer (etc.) mom and author, she couldn't be happier. Well, if she had a self-cleaning house, a Porsche, and an endless supply of chocolate-covered cinnamon bears, she just might be a *tad* bit happier. Visit her online at www.wendytoliver.com.

LOL at this sneak peek of

Love on Cue
By Catherine Hapka

A new Romantic Comedy from Simon Pulse

☆

I just stood there for a second gaping up at him in shock. Derek O'Malley. Here. At a Thespians party. Talking to me. I tried to form an answer to his question, but while my mouth moved, nothing came out. I probably looked like some kind of demented fish.

Luckily, Calla came to my rescue, as usual. "Come on in, handsome," she said into her karaoke microphone. For once she managed to be somewhat subtle as she shot me a quick, amused glance—I'm sure nobody else even noticed it, though of course I started blushing anyway. "I guess you heard we throw a rockin' party and just had to check it out for yourself, huh?"

Derek stepped into the room, seeming slightly confused. "Actually, I just wanted to talk to you guys."

I couldn't stop staring at him. Seeing him there just didn't compute. It was as if we'd been right in the middle of a performance

of, say, *Arsenic and Old Lace* and suddenly
Vladimir and Estragon from *Waiting for
Godot* had stepped onstage and started trading
existential banter. Or maybe it was more like
when the car radio got stuck halfway between
NPR and the Spanish-language station. No,
actually, it was weirder than that. It was as if
my secret daydreams had started leaking out
through my ears and turning into real life. I
could imagine the scientific studies now:

WORLD-FAMOUS SCIENTIST: Tell me,
Ms. Tannery, when did you first sus-
pect you could affect other people's
thoughts, feelings, and behavior
with the power of your mind?

ME: I remember the exact moment. It
was when Derek O'Malley walked
into a drama club party and declared
his undying love for me.

WFS: Hmm, I see.

DEREK, TO ME: Are you almost done
talking to the old coot in the white
lab coat, Maggie my beautiful
darling precious sweetheart lover?
Because if we don't start making
out within the next thirty seconds,
I shall die of a broken heart!

ME: Well, I certainly wouldn't want
    to be responsible for that . . . [*slurp,
    smooch*]

I blinked, trying to banish such thoughts. They were confusing me, and I didn't need that at the moment. I was already plenty bewildered enough. Most of the rest of the Thespians appeared to be almost as shocked as I was at Derek's unexpected entrance. And no wonder. Like every high school, Thornton had its different layers of social strata, and Derek belonged to a completely different one from the rest of us. He was practically a different species.

As usual, though, Calla was keeping her cool. "So here we are," she said. Leaning one dimpled elbow on top of Nico's largest speaker, she stared at Derek with open curiosity. "Talk to us."

Derek cleared his throat and came farther into the room. "Right," he said. "It's like this. I went down to Mexico with some buddies for break. We did some surfing while we were down there, and somehow I managed to mess up my knee pretty bad."

"Oh, but see, when we actors say 'break a leg,' we don't mean that literally," Duane said. "So there's no need to sue us over this, okay?"

Derek laughed along with everybody else. "I know, right?" he said sheepishly. "I feel like the world's biggest idiot for doing this right before baseball season."

"I don't get it," Tommy van Cleef called out in his usual blunt way. "What's this got to do with us? It's not like we care about baseball or sports or whatever."

"Well, like I was saying, baseball season's pretty much out for me this year." Derek shrugged. "But I always thought I might like to try acting, and now it looks like I've got some time on my hands. So I wanted to find out more about what I have to do to try out for your next show."

My heart skipped a beat. Derek O'Malley wanted to be in our play? The idea was both incredible and terrifying.

Meanwhile, some of the others were looking skeptical. "You mean you hurt your knee, and now you suddenly want to be an actor?" Glenn Thalberg asked. He's a senior who has been in every production of his high school career, and he's a little protective of the Thespians.

"Let me guess," Calla added. "College

apps need a bit more padding? Is that it?"

"No!" Derek said right away, shaking his head. "That's not it at all. Actually, my folks think I should use this time to, you know, focus on my studies or whatever. But like I said, I've always thought acting would be fun. I've been to see almost all your shows except during playoffs and stuff."

Wow. It was a good thing I hadn't known that at the time. It was one thing to perform in front of my friends, my family, my teachers, and everyone else I knew. But if I'd realized Derek O'Malley was sitting somewhere out in that darkened auditorium watching me, I probably would have fallen off the stage into the orchestra pit.

"Hmm." Calla crossed her arms over her chest. "He *sounds* sincere. But do we believe him?"

"I do!" Jenna Paolini put in with a giggle.

"Think about it this way, people. If he sounds sincere, it means one of two things," Rosalie Dibble spoke up, both as geeky and as logical as always. "Either he *is* sincere, or he's a good enough actor to fake it. Either way, it sounds like we should welcome him into our ranks."

"I don't know," Duane said. "If he really wants to act, maybe we ought to make him prove it—right here and now."

Nico rolled his eyes. "What's the big deal? It's an open audition, right? He doesn't need anyone's permission to try out."

"No, it's okay, man." Derek grinned. "I don't blame you guys for wanting to make sure I'm for real. What do you want me to do?"

"You may have heard our next show is *Romeo and Juliet*," Calla said. "Why don't you get up there and make like Romeo? That should let us see if you've got any chops."

There was a general murmur of agreement. "Maggie can run the lines with you," Tommy called out. "She knows the part."

Calla shot me a worried look. "No, wait, let me do it," she said quickly. "I mean, um, I want to be the one to see if Mr. Smooth Talker here has what it takes." She did the boom-boom thing and fluttered her eyelashes. Most people probably thought she was flirting her plus-size butt off with Derek, but I knew the truth. She was doing it for me. She realized that if I had to get up and play a romantic scene with Derek, I'd probably faint or throw up or something.

"Don't be greedy, Calla," Lizzy Paolini cried. "You already have a boyfriend."

"Maybe she's ready to trade up," her twin sister, Jenna, joked with a sly glance at Duane, who laughed and stuck out his tongue at her. "But anyway, Maggie's probably going to end up being Juliet, so *she* should totally do it."

Calla shrugged, and I gulped, feeling trapped and slightly queasy. Playing Juliet opposite Duane—or any other guy in the Thespians, or in the world, for that matter—was one thing. I could do that with both eyes shut and my script tied behind my back. But this? This was another thing entirely.

A million excuses scooted through my head. I could say my throat was sore. That I had to go to the bathroom. Or maybe I could just fake a sudden stroke. I was an actress, right? I could make it believable if I really tried. And nobody would even think about making me play Juliet in the ER.

But as usual, I wasn't able to react quickly enough to do any of those things. I just sort of froze and did nothing. And before I knew it, I found myself standing on the fake stage looking up at Derek.

At first I wasn't sure I could do it or

even survive the attempt. When I gazed up into Derek's handsome face, it was as if I'd been told I had to sing "The Star-Spangled Banner" stark naked in front of the entire population of Thornton High School. I just stood there, still frozen in place and feeling like I might hyperventilate. What was I supposed to do now? This wasn't how any of my daydreams about me and Derek had gone. . . .

Meanwhile, he wasn't even looking at me. "Yo, cut me a little slack here, okay?" he said to the others with a laugh. "I know we studied that play back in freshman year and all, but you don't really expect me to, like, start reciting it from memory, do you?"

"Well, I suppose you *are* a beginner . . . Here you go." Calla grabbed one of the scripts we'd left sitting on the speakers earlier and flipped through it. Handing it to Derek, she pointed to a spot. "Start right there, Romeo."

"Thanks." Derek glanced down at the script, then at me. The corners of his eyes crinkled in a completely adorable way as he winked and smiled. "Be gentle with me, okay?" he said softly. "I'm new to all this."

"O-okay," I managed to squeak out.

He took a deep breath and checked his script again. "Lady, by yonder blessed moon I vow, That tips with silver all these fruit-tree tops—"

"O, swear not by the moon, th' inconstant moon," I recited, my voice sounding as if it belonged to an asthmatic mouse. But somehow, in spite of the abject terror, my acting skills kicked in sort of automatically. By the second part of the line I sounded almost normal. "That monthly changes in her circled orb, Lest that thy love prove likewise variable."

"What shall I swear by?" Derek asked, his face radiating adoration. He was gazing at me as if we were the only two people in the room—in the world.

It was pretty overwhelming, but I also couldn't help being impressed. There was no trace of self-consciousness in his face or voice. He was just throwing himself into the part, bringing out the spirit of Romeo without even seeming to try. Still, he was a superstar at everything else he'd ever done. Why should it be a surprise that he could act, too?

We kept going, playing out the scene. Derek had to check his script a lot more often than I did, but he seemed to have the gist of how it went and what he was supposed to be feeling, so his lines rang true even when he stumbled over a word or phrase. And at some point everything sort of shifted, and just like that, it was as if we'd slid from reality into one of my fantasies, and the two of us really were alone beneath th' inconstant moon . . .

"O, wilt thou leave me so unsatisfied?" he asked throatily, reaching out and taking both my hands in his.

At his touch, it was as if a jolt of electricity passed between us, leaving me almost breathless. Judging by the way his blue eyes suddenly widened, he'd felt it too.

"What satisfaction canst thou have tonight?" I asked, our eyes locked together.

"Th' exchange of thy love's faithful vow for mine." His gaze was so intense that it felt like it was burning into me, right down to my soul. Before that moment, I'd always thought "weak in the knees" was just an expression. But now I knew exactly what it meant. I wondered what he would do if I collapsed into his arms. What would it feel like to have him catch me, hold me close with those strong arms? The thought was so distracting that I almost missed my next cue.

But I managed to pull it together, reciting my next few lines even while he stared at me as if he'd just discovered the meaning of life in my face. And somehow, in turn, it was as if Juliet's words and feelings became my own and just poured out of me naturally. I forgot about the rest of the Thespians watching, forgot to be self-conscious about performing in front of my dream guy, forgot everything except expressing what I was experiencing in that moment.

"My bounty is as boundless as the sea," I told Derek with an adoring sigh. "My love as deep; the more I give to thee, the more I have, for both are infinite."

He squeezed my hands in his, leaning closer until I could smell the clean scent of his aftershave. I could practically see the sparks flying between us. This wasn't movie-star daydream secret-fantasy kid stuff. This was *real*. The most amazing part was, I was pretty sure it was mutual. The way he was looking at me . . . you couldn't fake that, could you?

"Good night, good night!" I cried at last with a touch of desperation at the thought that we were almost finished. "Parting is such sweet sorrow, That I shall say good night till it be morrow."

And just like that, all too soon, the scene was over—and so was the magic.

"So?" Derek dropped my hands and turned toward the others with a grin. "What'd you think? Was that okay?"

Most of the Thespians applauded. A couple of girls gave loud wolf whistles as well, and Rosalie let out a genteel "Huzzah!"

"Not bad, not bad at all," Duane said. "I'd say you definitely won't embarrass yourself if you try out. Auditions start Thursday after school in the auditorium."

"Cool. I'll see you all there." Derek glanced back at me and smiled. "Hey, thanks for helping out, Maggie."

I'm not sure if I managed to reply before he left. My mind was filled with only one thought, better than all my fantasies rolled into one—he knew my name! Derek O'Malley, Mr. Perfect, my amazing Romeo, actually *knew who I was*!

Want to hear what the Romantic Comedies authors are doing when they are not writing books?

Check out PulseRoCom.com to see the authors blogging together, plus get sneak peeks of upcoming titles!

Even the tabloids
won't tell you the full story. . . .

The One

She'll do anything
to be famous

Ed Decter

The first book in a new trilogy by Ed Decter

From Simon Pulse
Published by Simon & Schuster

Need a distraction?

Julie Linker

Amy Belasen & Jacob Osborn

Anita Liberty

Lauren Baratz-Logsted

Teri Brown

Eileen Cook

Check Your Pulse

Simon & Schuster's **Check Your Pulse** e-newsletter offers current updates on the hottest titles, exciting sweepstakes, and exclusive content from your favorite authors.

Visit **SimonSaysTEEN.com** to sign up, post your thoughts, and find out what every avid reader is talking about!

Margaret K. McElderry Books

Simon & Schuster
Books for Young Readers

SIMON
PULSE